Vladimir Nabokov

Nabokov's Quartet

Panther

Granada Publishing Limited
First published in 1969 by Panther Books Limited
3 Upper James Street, London W1R 4BP

First published in Great Britain by
Weidenfeld & Nicolson Limited 1967
Panther edition published 1969
Reprinted 1972
Copyright © Vladimir Nabokov 1966
An Affair of Honor © 1966 The New Yorker Magazine
Inc.; *Lik* © 1964 The New Yorker Magazine Inc.;
The Vane Sisters © 1959 The Hudson Review; *The Visit
to the Museum* © 1963 Esquire Magazine.
Made and printed in Great Britain by
Richard Clay (The Chaucer Press), Ltd
Bungay, Suffolk
Set in Linotype Times 10/12 pt

Also by Vladimir Nabokov in Panther Books

Despair
The Defence
The Eye
The Gift

Contents

to Véra

Foreword

The four stories now offered to my readers span four decades of literary life. 'An Affair of Honor' appeared in the late nineteen twenties, in the émigré daily *Rul*, Berlin, and was included under the title *Podlets* (The Cur) in my first collection of stories ('*Vozvrashchenie Chorba*,' Slovo, Berlin, 1930). 'Lik' was published in the émigré review *Russkie zapiski*, Paris, February 1939, and in my third Russian collection ('*Vesna v Fialte*,' Chehov House, New York, 1956). 'The Visit to the Museum' (*Poseshchenie Muzeya*) appeared in the émigré review *Sovremennïe zapiski* No. 68, Paris, 1939, and in the 1956 collection. All three have been translated by my son Dmitri Nabokov into English and published in American periodicals ('The Visit to the Museum' in *Esquire*, March 1963; 'Lik' and 'An Affair of Honor' in *The New Yorker*, October 10, 1964, and September 1966, respectively). I wrote 'The Vane Sisters' in Ithaca, N.Y., in February 1959, in English. It appeared in *The Hudson Review*, Winter 1959, and in *Encounter*, March 1959.

'An Affair of Honor' renders, in a drab expatriate setting, the degradation of a romantic theme whose decline had started with Chehov's magnificent story *The Duel* (1891). 'Lik' reflects the miragy Riviera surroundings among which I composed it and attempts to create the impression of a stage performance engulfing a neurotic performer though not quite in the way that the trapped actor expected when dreaming of such an experience. Kafka and Kafkaesque shall not be dragged in by the student in connection with 'The Visit to the Museum,' and as usual Freudians should keep out. At one point in that story the unfortunate narrator notices a shop sign and realizes he is not in the Russia of his past but in the Russia of the Soviets: what gives it away is the absence of one letter which used to decorate the end of words after consonants but is now omitted in the re-formed orthography. Another narrator, the one of 'The Vane Sisters,' is supposed to be unaware that his last paragraph has been used acrostically by two dead girls to assert their mysterious participation in the story. This particular trick can be tried only once in a thousand years of fiction. Whether it has come off is another question.

VLADIMIR NABOKOV *Montreux March 10, 1966*

An Affair of Honor

1

The accursed day when Anton Petrovich made the acquaintance of Berg existed only in theory, for his memory had not affixed to it a date label at the time, and now it was impossible to identify that day. Broadly speaking, it happened last winter around Christmas 1926. Berg arose out of nonbeing, bowed in greeting, and settled down again—into an armchair instead of his previous nonbeing. It was at the Kurdyumovs', who lived on St. Mark Strasse, way off in the sticks, in the Moabit section of Berlin, I believe. The Kurdyumovs remained the paupers they had become after the Revolution, while Anton Petrovich and Berg, although also expatriates, had since grown somewhat richer. Now, when a dozen similar ties of a smoky, luminous shade—say that of a sunset cloud—appeared in a haberdasher's window, together with a dozen handkerchiefs in exactly the same tints, Anton Petrovich would buy both the fashionable tie and fashionable handkerchief, and every morning, on his way to the bank, would have the pleasure of encountering the same tie and the same handkerchief, worn by two or three gentlemen who were also hurrying to their offices. At one time he had business relations with Berg; Berg was indispensable, would call up five times a day, began frequenting their house, and would crack endless jokes—God, how he loved to crack jokes. The first time he came, Tanya, Anton Petrovich's wife, found that he resembled an Englishman and was very amusing. 'Hello, Anton!' Berg would roar, swooping down on Anton's hand, with outspread fingers (the way Russians do), and then shaking it vigorously. Berg was broad-

13

shouldered, well built, clean-shaven, and liked to compare himself to an athletic angel. He once showed Anton Petrovich a little old black notebook. The pages were all covered with crosses, exactly five hundred twenty-three in number. 'Civil war in the Crimea—a souvenir,' said Berg with a slight smile, and coolly added: 'Of course, I counted only those Reds I killed outright.' The fact that Berg was an ex-cavalry man and had fought under General Denikin aroused Anton Petrovich's envy, and he hated when Berg would tell, in front of Tanya, of reconnaissance forays and midnight attacks. Anton Petrovich himself was short-legged, rather plump, and wore a monocle, which, in its free time, when not screwed into his eye socket, dangled on a narrow black ribbon and, when Anton Petrovich sprawled in an easy chair, would gleam like a foolish eye on his belly. A boil, excised two years before, had left a scar on his left cheek. This scar as well as his coarse, cropped mustache and fat Russian nose, would twitch tensely when Anton Petrovich screwed the monocle home. 'Stop making faces,' Berg would say, 'you won't find an uglier one.'

In their glasses a light vapor floated over the tea; a half squashed chocolate eclair on a plate released its creamy inside; Tanya, her bare elbows resting on the table and her chin leaning on her interlaced fingers, gazed upwards at the drifting smoke of her cigarette, and Berg was trying to convince her that she must wear her hair short, that all women, from time immemorial, had done so, that the Venus de Milo had short hair, while Anton Petrovich heatedly and circumstantially objected, and Tanya only shrugged her shoulder, knocking the ash off her cigarette with a tap of her nail.

And then it all came to an end. One Wednesday at the end of July Anton Petrovich left for Kassel on business, and from there sent his wife a telegram that he would return on Friday. On Friday he found that he had to remain at least another week, and sent another telegram. On the following day, however, the deal fell through, and without bothering to wire a third time Anton Petrovich headed back to Berlin. He arrived about ten, tired and dissatisfied with his trip. From the street he saw that the bedroom windows of his flat were aglow, conveying the soothing news that his wife was at home. He went up to the fifth floor, with three twirls of the key unlocked the thrice locked door, and entered. As he passed through the front hall, he heard the steady noise of running water from the bathroom. 'Pink and moist,' Anton Petrovich thought with fond anticipation, and carried his bag on into the bedroom. In the bedroom, Berg was standing before the wardrobe mirror, putting on his tie.

Anton Petrovich mechanically lowered his little suitcase to the floor, without taking his eyes off Berg, who tilted up his impassive face, flipped back a bright length of tie and passed it through the knot. 'Above all, don't get excited,' said Berg, carefully tightening the knot. 'Please don't get excited. Stay perfectly calm.'

Must do something, Anton Petrovich thought, but what? He felt a tremor in his legs, an absence of legs—only that cold, aching tremor. Do something quick.... He started pulling a glove off one hand. The glove was new and fit snugly. Anton Petrovich kept jerking his head and muttering mechanically, 'Go away immediately. This is dreadful. Go away....'

'I'm going, I'm going, Anton,' said Berg, squaring his broad shoulders as he leisurely got into his jacket.

'If I hit him, he'll hit me too,' Anton Petrovich thought in a flash. He pulled off the glove with a final yank and threw it awkwardly at Berg. The glove slapped against the wall and dropped into the washstand pitcher.

'Good shot,' said Berg.

He took his hat and cane, and headed past Anton Petrovich toward the door. 'All the same, you'll have to let me out,' he said. 'The downstairs door is locked.'

Scarcely aware of what he was doing Anton Petrovich followed him out. As they started to go down the stairs, Berg, who was in front, suddenly began to laugh. 'Sorry,' he said without turning his head, 'but this is awfully funny—being kicked out with such complications.' At the next landing he chuckled again and accelerated his step. Anton Petrovich also quickened his pace. That dreadful rush was unseemly ... Berg was deliberately making him go down in leaps and bounds. What torture.... Third floor ... second.... When will these stairs end? Berg flew down the remaining steps and stood waiting for Anton Petrovich, lightly tapping the floor with his cane. Anton Petrovich was breathing heavily, and had trouble getting the dancing key into the trembling lock. At last it opened.

'Try not to hate me,' said Berg from the sidewalk. 'Put yourself in my place....'

Anton Petrovich slammed the door. From the very beginning he had had a ripening urge to slam some door or other. The noise made his ears ring. Only now, as he climbed the stairs, did he realize that his face was wet with tears. As he passed through the front hall, he heard again the noise of running water. Hopefully waiting for the tepid to grow hot. But now above that noise he could also hear Tanya's voice. She was singing loudly in the bathroom.

With an odd sense of relief, Anton Petrovich returned to the bedroom. He now saw what he had not noticed before—that both beds were tumbled and that a pink nightgown lay on his wife's. Her new evening dress and a pair of silk stockings were laid out on the sofa: evidently, she was getting ready to go dancing with Berg. Anton Petrovich took his expensive fountain pen out of his breast pocket. I cannot bear to see you. I cannot trust myself if I see you. He wrote standing up, bending awkwardly over the dressing table. His monocle was blurred by a large tear ... the letters swam.... Please go away. I am leaving you some cash. I'll talk it over with Natasha tomorrow. Sleep at her house or at a hotel tonight—only please do not stay here. He finished writing and placed the paper against the mirror, in a spot where she would be sure to see it. Beside it he put a hundred-mark note. And, passing through the front hall, he again heard his wife singing in the bathroom. She had a gypsy kind of voice, a bewitching voice ... happiness, a summer night, a guitar ... she sang that night seated on a cushion in the middle of the floor, and slitted her smiling eyes as she sang.... He had just proposed to her ... yes, happiness, a summer night, a moth bumping against the ceiling, 'my soul I surrender to you, I love you with infinite passion....' 'How dreadful! How dreadful!' he kept repeating as he walked down the street. The night was very mild, with a swarm of stars. It did not matter which way he went. By now she had probably come out of the

17

bathroom and found the note. Anton Petrovich winced as he remembered the glove. A brand-new glove afloat in a brimming pitcher. The vision of this brown wretched thing caused him to utter a cry that made a passerby start. He saw the dark shapes of huge poplars around a square and thought, 'Mityushin lives here someplace.' Anton Petrovich called him up from a bar, which arose before him as in a dream and then receded into the distance like the tail light of a train. Mityushin let him in but he was drunk, and at first paid no attention to Anton Petrovich's livid face. A person unknown to Anton Petrovich sat in the small dim room, and a black-haired lady in a red dress lay on the couch with her back to the table, apparently asleep. Bottles gleamed on the table. Anton Petrovich had arrived in the middle of a birthday celebration, but he never understood whether it was being held for Mityushin, the fair sleeper or the unknown man (who turned out to be a Russified German with the strange name of Gnuschke). Mityushin, his rosy face beaming, introduced him to Gnushke, and, indicating with a nod the generous back of the sleeping lady, remarked casually, 'Adelaida Albertovna, I want you to meet a great friend of mine.' The lady did not stir; Mityushin, however, did not show the least surprise, as if he had never expected her to wake up. All of this was a little bizarre and nightmarish—that empty vodka bottle with a rose stuck into its neck, that chess board on which a higgledy piggledy game was in progress, the sleeping lady, the drunken, but quite peaceful Gnuschke. . . .

'Have a drink,' said Mityushin, and then suddenly raised his eyebrows. 'What's the matter with you, Anton Petrovich. You look very ill.'

'Yes, by all means, have a drink,' with idiotic earnestness said Gnuschke, a very long-faced man in a very tall collar, who resembled a dachshund.

Anton Petrovich gulped down half a cup of vodka and sat down.

'Now tell us what's happened,' said Mityushin. 'Don't be embarrassed in front of Henry—he is the most honest man on earth. My move, Henry, and I warn you, if after this you grab my bishop, I'll mate you in three moves. Well, out with it, Anton Petrovich.'

'We'll see about that in a minute,' said Gnuschke, revealing a big starched cuff as he stretched out his arm. 'You forgot about the pawn at h5.'

'H5 yourself,' said Mityushin. 'Anton Petrovich is going to tell us his story.'

Anton Petrovich had some more vodka and the room went into a spin. The gliding chessboard seemed on the point to collide with the bottles; the bottles, together with the table, set off toward the couch; the couch with mysterious Adelaida Albertovna headed for the window; and the window also started to move. This accursed motion was somehow connected with Berg, and had to be stopped—stopped at once, trampled upon, torn, destroyed. . . .

'I want you to be my second,' began Anton Petrovich, and was dimly aware that the phrase sounded oddly truncated but could not correct that flaw.

'Second what?' said Mityushin absently, glancing askance at the chessboard, over which Gnuschke's hand hung its fingers wriggling.

'No, you listen to me,' Anton Petrovich exclaimed with anguish in his voice. 'You just listen! Let us not drink any more. This is serious, very serious.'

Mityushin fixed him with his shiny blue eyes. 'The game is cancelled, Henry,' he said, without looking at Gnuschke. 'This sounds serious.'

'I intend to fight a duel,' whispered Anton Petrovich, trying by mere optical force to hold back the table that kept floating away. 'I wish to kill a certain person. His name is Berg—You may have met him at my place. I prefer not to explain my reasons....'

'You can explain everything to your second,' said Mityushin smugly.

'Excuse me for interfering,' said Gnuschke suddenly, and raised his index finger. 'Remember, it has been said: "Thou shalt not kill!"'

'The man's name is Berg,' said Anton Petrovich. 'I think you know him. And I need two seconds.' The ambiguity could be now ignored.

'A duel,' said Gnuschke.

Mityushin nudged him with his elbow. 'Don't interrupt, Henry.'

'And that is all,' Anton Petrovich concluded in a whisper and, lowering his eyes, feebly fingered the ribbon of his totally useless monocle.

Silence. The lady on the couch snored comfortably. A car passed in the street, its horn blaring.

'I'm drunk, and Henry's drunk,' muttered Mityushin, 'but apparently something very serious has happened.' He chewed on his knuckles and looked at Gnuschke. 'What do you think, Henry?' Gnuschke sighed.

'Tomorrow you two will call on him,' said Anton Petrovich. 'Select the spot, and so on. He did not leave me his card. According to the rules he should have given me his card. I threw my glove at him.'

'You are acting like a noble and courageous man,' said Gnuschke with growing animation. 'By a strange coincidence, I am not unfamiliar with these matters. A cousin of mine was also killed in a duel.'

'Why "also?"' Anton Petrovich wondered in anguish. 'Can this be a portent?'

Mityushin took a swallow from his cup and said jauntily:

'As a friend, I cannot refuse. We'll go see Mr. Berg in the morning.'

'As far as the German laws are concerned,' said Gnuschke, 'If you kill him, they'll put you in jail for several years; if, on the other hand, you are killed, they won't bother you.'

'I have taken all that into consideration,' Anton Petrovich said solemnly.

Then there appeared again that beautiful expensive implement, that shiny black pen with its delicate gold nib, which in normal times would glide like a wand of velvet across the paper; now, however, Anton Petrovich's hand shook, and the table heaved like the deck of a storm-tossed ship.... On a sheet of foolscap that Mityushin produced, Anton Petrovich wrote a cartel of defiance to Berg, three times calling him a scoundrel and concluding with the lame sentence: "One of us mush perish." '

Having done, he burst into tears, and Gnuschke, clucking his tongue, wiped the poor fellow's face with a large red-checked handkerchief, while Mityushin kept pointing at the chessboard, repeating ponderously, 'You finish him off like that king there—mate in three moves and no questions asked.' Anton Petrovich sobbed, and tried to brush away Gnuschke's friendly hands, repeating with childish intonations 'I loved her so much, so much!'

And a new sad day was dawning.

'So at nine you will be at his house,' said Anton Petrovich, lurching out of his chair.

'At nine we'll be at his house,' Gnuschke replied like an echo.

'We'll get in five hours of sleep,' said Mityushin.

Anton Petrovich smoothed his hat into shape (he had been sitting on it all the while), caught Mityushin's hand, held it for a moment, lifted it and pressed it to his cheek.

'Come, come, you shouldn't,' mumbled Mityushin and, as before, addressed the sleeping lady, 'Our friend is leaving, Adelaida Albertovna.'

This time she stirred, awakened with a start, and turned over heavily. Her face was full and creased by sleep, with slanting, excessively made-up eyes. 'You fellows better stop drinking,' she said calmly, and turned back toward the wall.

At the corner of the street Anton Petrovich found a sleepy taxi, which whisked him with ghostly speed through the wastes of the blue-gray city and fell again asleep in front of his house. In the front hall he met Elspeth the maid, who opened her mouth and looked at him with unkind eyes, as if about to say something; but she thought better of it, and shuffled off down the corridor in her carpet slippers.

'Wait,' said Anton Petrovich. 'Is my wife gone?'

'It's shameful,' the maid said with great emphasis. 'This is a madhouse. Lug trunks in the middle of the night, turn everything upside down. . . .'

'I asked if my wife was gone,' Anton Petrovich shouted in a high-pitched voice.

'She is,' glumly answered Elspeth.

Anton Petrovich went on into the parlor. He decided to sleep there. The bedroom, of course, was out of the question. He turned on the light, lay down on the sofa, and covered himself with his overcoat. For some reason his left wrist felt uncomfortable. Oh, of course—my watch. He took it off and wound it, thinking at the same time. 'Extraordinary, how this man retains his composure—does not even forget to wind his watch.' And, since he was still drunk, enormous, rhythmic waves immediately began rocking him, up and down, up and down, and he began to feel very sick. He sat up ... the big copper ashtray ... quick.... His insides gave such a heave that a pain shot through his groin ... and it all missed the ashtray. He fell asleep right away. One foot, in its black shoe and gray spat dangled from the couch, and the light (which he had quite forgotten to turn off) lent a pale gloss to his sweaty forehead.

2

Mityushin was a brawler and a drunkard. He could go and do all kinds of things at the least provocation. A real daredevil. One also recalls having heard about a certain friend of his who, to spite the post office, used to throw lighted matches into mailboxes. He was nicknamed the Gnut. Quite possibly it was Gnuschke. Actually, all Anton Petrovich had intended to do was to spend the night at Mityushin's place. Then, suddenly, for no reason at all that talk about duels had started. ... Oh, of course Berg must be killed; only the matter ought to have been carefully thought out first, and, if it had come to choosing seconds, they should in any case have been gentlemen. As it was, the whole thing had taken on an absurd, improper turn. Everything had been absurd and improper—beginning with the glove and ending with the ashtray. But now, of course, there was nothing to be done about it—he would have to drain this cup. ...

He felt under the couch, where his watch had landed. Eleven. Mityushin and Gnuschke have already been at Berg's. Suddenly a pleasant thought darted among the others, pushed them apart, and disappeared. What was it? Oh, of course! They had been drunk yesterday, and he had been drunk too. They must have overslept, then come to their senses and thought that he had been babbling nonsense; but the pleasant thought flashed past and vanished. It made no difference—the thing had been started and he would have to repeat to them what he had said yesterday. Still it was odd that they had not shown up yet. A duel. What an impressive word 'duel'! I am having a duel. Hostile meeting. Single combat. Duel.

'Duel' sounds best. He got up, and noticed that his trousers were terribly wrinkled. The ashtray had been removed. Elspeth must have come in while he was sleeping. How embarrassing. Must go see how things look in the bedroom. Forget his wife. She did not exist any more. Never had existed. All of that was gone. Anton Petrovich took a deep breath and opened the bedroom door. He found the maid there stuffing a crumpled newspaper into the wastebasket.

'Bring me some coffee, please,' he said, and went to the dressing table. There was an envelope on it. His name; Tanya's hand. Beside it, in disorder, lay his hairbrush, his comb, his shaving brush, and an ugly, stiff glove. Anton Petrovich opened the envelope. The hundred marks and nothing else. He turned it this way and that, not knowing what to do with it.

'Elspeth. . . .'

The maid approached, glancing at him suspiciously.

'Here, take it. You were put to so much inconvenience last night, and then those other unpleasant things. . . . Go on, take it.'

'One hundred marks?' the maid asked in a whisper, and then suddenly blushed crimson. Heaven only knows what rushed through her head, but she banged the wastebasket down on the floor and shouted, 'No! You can't bribe me, I'm an honest woman. Just you wait, I'll tell everybody you wanted to bribe me. No! This is a madhouse. . . .' And she went out, slamming the door.

'What's wrong with her? Good Lord, what's wrong with her?' muttered Anton Petrovich in confusion, and, stepping rapidly to the door, shrieked after the maid, 'Get out this minute, get out of this house!'

'That's the third person I've thrown out,' he thought, his whole body trembling. 'And now there is no one to bring me my coffee.'

He spent a long time washing and changing, and then sat in the café across the street, glancing every so often to see if Mityushin and Gnuschke were not coming. He had lots of business to attend to in town, but he could not be bothered with business. Duel. A glamorous word.

In the afternoon Natasha, Tanya's sister, dropped in. She was so upset that she could barely speak. Anton Petrovich paced back and forth, giving little pats to the furniture. Tanya had arrived at her sister's flat in the middle of the night, in a terrible state, a state you simply could not imagine. Anton Petrovich suddenly found it strange to be saying '*ty*' (thou) to Natasha. After all, he was no longer married to her sister.

'I shall give her a certain sum every month under certain conditions,' he said, trying to keep a rising hysterical note out of his voice.

'Money isn't the point,' answered Natasha, sitting in front of him and swinging her glossily stockinged leg. 'The point is that this is an absolutely awful mess.'

'Thanks for coming,' said Anton Petrovich, 'we'll have another chat some time, only right now I'm very busy.' As he saw her to the door, he remarked casually (or at least he hoped it sounded casual), 'I'm fighting a duel with him.' Natasha's lips quivered; she quickly kissed him on the cheek and went out. How strange that she did not start imploring him not to fight. By all rights she ought to have implored him not to fight. In our time nobody fights duels. She is wearing the same perfume as. . . . As who? No, no, he had never been married.

A little later still, at about seven, Mityushin and Gnuschke arrived. They looked grim. Gnuschke bowed with reserve and handed Anton Petrovich a sealed business envelope. He opened it. It began: 'I have received your extremely stupid and extremely rude message. . . .' Anton Petrovich's monocle fell out, he reinserted it. 'I feel very sorry for you, but since you have adopted this attitude, I have no choice but to accept your challenge. Your seconds are pretty awful. Berg.'

Anton Petrovich's throat went unpleasantly dry, and there was again that ridiculous quaking in his legs.

'Sit down, sit down,' he said, and himself sat down first. Gnuschke sank back into an armchair, caught himself, and sat up on its edge.

'He's a highly insolent character,' Mityushin said with feeling. 'Imagine—he kept laughing all the while, so that I nearly punched him in the teeth.'

Gnuschke cleared his throat and said, 'There is only one thing I can advise you to do: take careful aim, because he is also going to take careful aim.'

Before Anton Petrovich's eyes flashed a notebook page covered with X's: diagram of a cemetery.

'He is a dangerous fellow,' said Gnuschke, leaning back in his armchair, sinking again, and again wriggling out.

'Who's going to make the report, Henry, you or I?' asked Mityushin, chewing on a cigarette as he jerked at his lighter with his thumb.

'You'd better do it,' said Gnuschke.

'We've had a very busy day,' began Mityushin, goggling his baby-blue eyes at Anton Petrovich. 'At exactly eight-thirty Henry, who was still as tight as a drum, and I. . . .'

'I protest,' said Gnuschke.

'. . . went to call on Mr. Berg. He was sipping his coffee. Right off we handed him your little note. Which he read. And what did he do, Henry? Yes, he burst out laughing. We waited for him to finish laughing, and Henry asked what his plans were.'

'No, not his plans, but how he intended to react,' Gnuschke corrected.

'. . . to react. To this, Mr. Berg replied that he agreed to fight and that he chose pistols. We have settled all the conditions: The combatants will be placed facing each other at twenty paces. Firing will be regulated by a word of command. If nobody is dead after the first exchange, the duel may go on. And on. What else was there, Henry?'

'If it is impossible to procure real dueling pistols, then Browning automatics will be used,' said Gnuschke.

'Browning automatics. Having established this much, we asked Mr. Berg how to get in touch with his seconds. He went out to telephone. Then he wrote the letter you have before you. Incidentally, he kept joking all the time. The next thing we did was to go to a café to meet his two chums. I bought Gnuschke a carnation for his button-hole. It was by this carnation that they recognized us. They introduced themselves, and, well, to put it in a nut-shell, everything is in order. Their names are Marx and Engels.'

'That's not quite exact,' interjected Gnuschke. 'They are Markov and Colonel Arkhangelski.'

'No matter,' said Mityushin and went on. 'Here begins

the epic part. We went out of town with these chaps to look for a suitable spot. You know Weissdorf, just beyond Wannsee. That's it. We took a walk through the woods there and found a glade, where, it turned out, these chaps had had a little picnic with their girls the other day. The glade is small, and all around there is nothing but woods. In short, the ideal spot—although, of course, you don't get the grand mountain decor as in Lermontov's fatal affair. See the state of my boots—all white with dust.'

'Mine too,' said Gnuschke. 'I must say that trip was quite a strenuous one.'

There followed a pause.

'It's hot today,' said Mityushin. 'Even hotter than yesterday.'

'Considerably hotter,' said Gnuschke.

With exaggerated thoroughness Mityushin began crushing his cigarette in the ashtray. Silence. Anton Petrovich's heart was beating in his throat. He tried to swallow it, but it started pounding even harder. When would the duel take place? Tomorrow? Why didn't they tell him? Maybe the day after tomorrow? It would be better the day after tomorrow. . . .

Mityushin and Gnuschke exchanged glances and got up.

'We shall call for you tomorrow at six-thirty A.M.,' said Mityushin. 'There is no point in leaving sooner. There isn't a damn soul out there anyway.'

Anton Petrovich got up too. What should he do? Thank them?

'Well, thank you, gentlemen. . . . Thank you, gentlemen. . . . Everything is settled, then. All right, then.'

The others bowed.

'We must still find a doctor and the pistols,' said Gnuschke.

In the front hall Anton Petrovich took Mityushin by the elbow and mumbled, 'You know, it's awfully silly, but you see, I don't know how to shoot, so to speak, I mean, I know how, but I've had no practice at all. . . .'

'Hm,' said Mityushin, 'that's too bad. Today is Sunday, otherwise you could have taken a lesson or two. That's really bad luck.'

'Colonel Arkhangelski gives private shooting lessons,' put in Gnuschke.

'Yes,' said Mityushin. 'You're the smart one, aren't you? Still, what are we to do, Anton Petrovich? You know what—beginners are lucky. Put your trust in God and just press the trigger.'

They left. Dusk was falling. Nobody had lowered the blinds. There must be some cheese and graham bread in the sideboard. The rooms were deserted and motionless, as if all the furniture had once breathed and moved about but had now died. A ferocious cardboard dentist bending over a panic-stricken patient of cardboard—this he had seen such a short time ago, on a blue, green, violet, ruby night, shot with fireworks, at the Luna Amusement Park. Berg took a long time aiming, the air rifle popped, the pellet hit the target, releasing a spring, and the cardboard dentist yanked out a huge tooth with a quadruple root. Tanya clapped her hands, Anton Petrovich smiled, Berg fired again, and the cardboard discs rattled as they spun, the clay pipes were shattered one after another, and the ping-pong ball dancing on a slender jet of water disappeared. How awful. . . . And, most awful of all, Tanya had then said jokingly, 'It wouldn't be much fun fighting a duel with you.' Twenty paces. Anton Petrovich went from door to window, counting the paces. Eleven. He inserted his monocle, and tried to estimate the distance. Two such rooms. Oh, if only he could manage to disable Berg at the first fire. But he did not know how to aim the thing. He was bound to miss. Here, this letter opener, for example. No, better take this paperweight. You are supposed to hold it like this and take aim. Or like this, perhaps, right up near your chin—it seems easier to do it this way. And at this instant, as he held before him the paperweight in the form of a parrot, pointing it this way and that, Anton Petrovich realized that he would be killed.

At about ten he decided to go to bed. The bedroom, though, was taboo. With great effort he found some clean bedclothes in the dresser, recased the pillow, and spread a sheet over the leather couch in the parlor. As he undressed, he thought, 'I am going to bed for the last time in my life.' 'Nonsense,' faintly squeaked some little particle of Anton Petrovich's soul, the same particle that had made him throw the glove, slam the door, and call Berg a scoundrel. 'Nonsense!' Anton Petrovich said in a thin voice, and at once told himself it was not right to say such things. If I think that nothing will happen to me, then the worst will happen. Everything in life always happens the other way around. It would be nice to read something—for the last time—before going to sleep.

'There I go again,' he moaned inwardly. 'Why for the last time? I am in a terrible state. I must take hold of myself. Oh, if only I were given some sign. Cards?'

He found a deck of cards on a nearby console and

took the top card, a three of diamonds. What does the three of diamonds mean chiromantically? No idea. Then he drew, in that order, the queen of diamonds, the eight of clubs, the ace of spades. Ah! That's bad. The ace of spades—I think that means death. But then that's a lot of nonsense, superstitious nonsense.... Midnight. Five past. Tomorrow has become today. I have a duel today.

He sought peace in vain. Strange things kept happening: the book he was holding, a novel by some German writer or other, was called *The Magic Mountain*, and mountain, in German, is 'Berg'; he decided that if he counted to three and a streetcar went by at 'three' he would be killed, and a streetcar obliged. And then Anton Petrovich did the very worst thing a man in his situation could have done: he decided to reason out what death really meant. When he had thought along these lines for a minute or so, everything lost sense. He found it difficult to breathe. He got up, walked about the room, and took a look out the window at the pure and terrible night sky. 'Must write my testament,' thought Anton Petrovich. But to make a will was, so to speak, playing with fire; it meant inspecting the contents of one's own urn in the columbarium. 'Best thing is to get some sleep,' he said aloud. But as soon as he closed his eyelids, Berg's grinning face would appear before him, purposively slitting one eye. He would turn on the light again, attempt to read, smoke, though he was not a regular smoker. Trivial memories floated by—a toy pistol, a path in the park, that sort of thing—and he would immediately cut short his recollections with the thought that those who are about to die always remember trifles from their past.

Then the opposite thing frightened him: he realized that he was not thinking of Tanya, that he was numbed by a strange drug that made him insensitive to her absence. She was my life and she has gone, he thought. I have already, unconsciously, bid life farewell, and everything is now indifferent to me, since I shall be killed.... The night, meanwhile, was beginning to wane.

At about four he shuffled into the dining room and drank a glass of soda water. A mirror near which he passed reflected his striped pajamas, and thinning, wispy hair. 'I'm going to look like my own ghost ...,' he thought. 'But how can I get some sleep? How?'

He wrapped himself in a lap robe, for he noticed that his teeth were chattering, and sat down in an armchair in the middle of the dim room that was slowly ascertaining itself. How will it all be? I must dress soberly, but elegantly. Tuxedo? No, that would be idiotic. A black suit, then ... and, yes, a black tie. The new black suit. But if there's a wound, a shoulder wound, say.... The suit will be ruined.... The blood, the hole, and, besides, they may start cutting off the sleeve. Nonsense, nothing of the sort is going to happen. I must wear my new black suit. And when the duel starts, I shall turn up my jacket collar—that's the custom, I think, in order to conceal the whiteness of one's shirt, probably, or simply because of the morning damp. That's how they did it in that film I saw. Then I must keep absolutely cool, and address everyone politely and calmly. Thank you, I have already fired. It is your turn now. If you do not remove that cigarette from your mouth I shall not fire. I am ready to continue. 'Thank you, I have already laughed'—that's what you say to a stale joker.... Oh, if one could only imagine all the details! They would arrive—he, Mityu-shin and Gnuschke—in a car, leave the car on the road, walk into the woods. Berg and his seconds would prob-ably be waiting there already, they always do in books. Now, there was a question: Does one salute one's oppo-nent? What does Onegin do in the opera? Perhaps a discreet tip of the hat from a distance would be just right. Then they would probably start marking off the yards and loading the pistols. What would he do mean-while? Yes, of course—he would place one foot on a stump somewhere a little way off, and wait in a casual attitude. But what if Berg also put one foot on a stump? Berg was capable of it.... Mimicking me to embarrass me. That would be awful. Other possibilities would be to lean against a tree trunk, or simply sit down on the grass. Somebody (in a Pushkin story?) ate cherries from a paper bag. Yes, but you have to bring that bag to the dueling ground—looks silly. Oh, well, he would decide when the time came. Dignified and nonchalant. Then we would take our positions. Twenty yards between us. It would be then that he should turn up his collar. He would grasp the pistol like this. Colonel Angel would wave a handkerchief or count till three. And then, sud-denly, something utterly terrible, something absurd would happen—an unimaginable thing, even if one thought about it for nights on end, even if one lived to be a hundred in Turkey.... Nice to travel, sit in cafés.... What does one feel when a bullet hits you between the ribs or in the forehead? Pain? Nausea? Or is there simply a bang followed by total darkness? The tenor Sobinov once crashed down so realistically that his pistol flew into the orchestra. And what if, instead, he received a ghastly wound of some kind—in one eye, or in the groin? No, Berg would kill him outright. Of course, here I've counted only the ones I killed outright. One more cross in that little black book. Unimaginable. . . .

The dining-room clock struck five: Ding-dawn. With a tremendous effort, shivering and clutching at the lap robe, Anton Petrovich got up, then paused again, lost in thought and suddenly stamped his foot, as Louis XVI stamped his when told it was time, Your Majesty, to go to the scaffold. Nothing to be done about it. Stamped his soft clumsy foot. The execution was inevitable. Time to shave, wash, and dress. Scrupulously clean underwear, and the new black suit. As he inserted the opal links into his shirt cuffs, Anton Petrovich mused that opals were the stones of fate and that it was only two or three hours before the shirt would be all bloody. Where would the hole be? He stroked the shiny hairs that went down his fat warm chest, and felt so frightened that he covered his eyes with his hand. There was something pathetically independent about the way everything within him was moving now—the heart pulsating, the lungs swelling, the blood circulating, the intestines contracting—and he was leading to slaughter this tender, defenseless, inner creature, that lived so blindly, so trustingly. . . . Slaughter! He grabbed his favorite shirt, undid one button and grunted as he plunged head first into the cold, white darkness of the linen enveloping him. Socks, tie. He awkwardly shined his shoes with a chamois rag. As he searched for a clean handkerchief he stumbled on a stick of rouge. He glanced into the mirror at his hideously pale face, and then tentatively touched his cheek with the crimson stuff. At first it made him look even worse than before. He licked his finger and rubbed his cheek, regretting that he had never taken a close look at how women apply make-up. A light, brick hue was finally imparted to his cheeks, and he decided it looked all right. 'There, I'm ready now,' he said, addressing the mirror; then came an agonizing yawn, and the mirror dissolved into tears. He rapidly scented his handkerchief, distributed papers, handkerchief, keys, and fountain pen in various pockets, and slipped into the black noose of his monocle. Pity I don't have a good pair of gloves. The pair I had was nice and new, but the left glove is widowed. The drawback inherent in duels. He sat down at his writing desk, placed his elbows on it, and began waiting, glancing now out the window, now at the traveling clock in its folding leather case.

It was a beautiful morning. The sparrows twittered like mad in the tall linden tree under the window. A pale-blue, velvet shadow covered the street, and here and there a roof would flash silver. Anton Petrovich was cold and had an unbearable headache. A nip of brandy would be paradise. None in the house. House already deserted; master going away forever. Oh, nonsense. We insist on calmness. The front door bell will ring in a moment. I must keep perfectly calm. The bell is going to ring right now. They are already three minutes late. Maybe they won't come? Such a marvelous summer morning.... Who was the last person killed in a duel in Russia? A Baron Manteuffel, twenty years ago. No, they won't come. Good. He would wait another half-hour, and then go to bed—the bedroom was losing its horror and becoming definitely attractive. Anton Petrovich opened his mouth wide, preparing to squeeze out a huge lump of yawn—he felt the crunch in his ears, the swelling under his palate—and it was then that the door bell brutally rang. Spasmodically swallowing the unfinished yawn, Anton Petrovich went into the front hall, unlocked the door, and Mityushin and Gnuschke ushered each other across the threshold.

'Time to go,' said Mityushin, gazing intently at Anton Petrovich. He was wearing his usual pistachio-colored tie, but Gnuschke had put on an old frockcoat.

'Yes, I am ready,' said Anton Petrovich, 'I'll be right with you. . . .'

He left them standing in the front hall, rushed into the bedroom, and, in order to gain time, started washing his hands, while he kept repeating to himself 'What is happening? My God, what is happening?' Just five minutes ago there had still been hope, there might have been an earthquake, Berg might have died of a heart attack, fate might have intervened, suspended events, saved him.

'Anton Petrovich, hurry up,' called Mityushin from the front hall. Quickly he dried his hands and joined the others.

'Yes, yes, I'm ready, let's go.'

'We'll have to take the train,' said Mityushin when they were outside. 'Because if we arrive by taxi in the middle of the forest, and at this hour, it might seem suspicious, and the driver might tell the police. Anton Petrovich, please don't start losing your nerve.'

'I'm not—don't be silly,' replied Anton Petrovich with a helpless smile.

Gnuschke, who had remained silent until this point, loudly blew his nose and said matter-of-factly:

'Our adversary is bringing the doctor. We were unable to find dueling pistols. However, our colleagues did procure two identical Brownings.'

In the taxi that was to take them to the station, they seated themselves thus: Anton Petrovich and Mityushin in back, and Gnuschke facing them on the jump seat, with his legs pulled in. Anton Petrovich was again overcome by a nervous fit of yawning. That revengeful yawn he had suppressed. Again and again came that humpy spasm, so that his eyes watered. Mityushin and Gnuschke looked very solemn, but at the same time seemed exceedingly pleased with themselves.

Anton Petrovich clenched his teeth and yawned with his nostrils only. Then, abruptly, he said, 'I had an excellent night's sleep.' He tried to think of something else to say....

'Quite a few people in the streets,' he said, and added, 'In spite of the early hour.' Mityushin and Gnuschke were silent. Another fit of yawning. Oh, God....

They soon arrived at the station. It seemed to Anton Petrovich that he had never traveled so fast. Gnuschke bought the tickets, and, holding them fanwise, went ahead. Suddenly he looked around at Mityushin and cleared his throat significantly. By the refreshment booth stood Berg. He was getting some change out of his trouser pocket, thrusting his left hand deep inside it, and holding the pocket in place with his right, the way Anglo-Saxons do in cartoons. He produced a coin in the palm of his hand, and, as he handed it to the woman vendor, said something that made her laugh. Berg laughed too. He stood with legs slightly spread. He was wearing a gray flannel suit.

'Let's go around that booth,' said Mityushin. 'It would be awkward passing right next to him.'

A strange numbness came over Anton Petrovich. Totally unconscious of what he was doing, he boarded the coach, took a window seat, removed his hat, donned it again. Only when the train jerked and began to move did his brain start working again, and in this instant he was possessed by the feeling that comes in dreams when, speeding along in a train from nowhere to nowhere, you suddenly realize that you are traveling clad only in your underpants.

'They are in the next coach,' said Mityushin, taking out a cigarette case. 'Why on earth do you keep yawning all the time, Anton Petrovich? It gives one the creeps.'

'I always do in the morning,' mechanically answered Anton Petrovich.

Pine trees, pine trees, pine trees. A sandy slope. More pine trees. Such a marvelous morning. . . .

'That frockcoat, Henry, is not a success,' said Mityushin. 'No question about it—to put it bluntly—it just isn't.'

'That is my business,' said Gnuschke.

Lovely, those pines. And now a gleam of water. Woods again. How touching, the world, how fragile. . . . If I could only keep from yawning again . . . jaws aching. If you restrain the yawn, your eyes begin watering. He was sitting with his face turned toward the window, listening to the wheels beating out the rhythm 'Abattoir . . . abattoir . . . abattoir. . . .'

'Here's what I advise you to do,' said Gnuschke. 'Blaze at once. I advise you to aim at the center of his body—you have more of a chance that way.'

'It's all a question of luck,' said Mityushin. 'If you hit him, fine, and if not, don't worry—he might miss too. A duel becomes real only after the first exchange. It is then that the interesting part begins, so to speak.'

A station. Did not stop long. Why did they torture him so? To die today would be unthinkable. What if I faint? You have to be a good actor.... What can I try? What shall I do? Such a marvelous morning....

'Anton Petrovich, excuse me for asking,' said Mityushin, 'but it's important. You don't have anything to entrust to us? I mean, papers, documents. A letter, maybe, or a will? It's the usual procedure.'

Anton Petrovich shook his head.

'Pity,' said Mityushin. 'Never know what might happen. Take Henry and me—we're all set for a sojourn in jail. Are your affairs in order?'

Anton Petrovich nodded. He was no longer able to speak. The only way to keep from screaming was to watch the pines that kept flashing past.

'We get off in a minute,' said Gnuschke, and rose. Mityushin rose also. Clenching his teeth, Anton Petrovich wanted to rise too, but a jolt of the train made him fall back into his seat.

'Here we are,' said Mityushin.

Only then did Anton Petrovich manage to separate himself from the seat. Pressing his monocle into his eye socket, he cautiously descended to the platform. The sun welcomed him warmly.

'They are behind,' said Gnuschke. Anton Petrovich felt his back growing a hump. No, this is unthinkable, I must wake up.

They left the station and set out along the highway,

past tiny brick houses with petunias in the windows. There was a tavern at the intersection of the highway and of a soft, white road leading off into the forest. Suddenly Anton Petrovich stopped.

'I'm awfully thirsty,' he muttered. 'I could do with a drop of something.'

'Yes, wouldn't hurt,' said Mityushin. Gnuschke looked back and said, 'They have left the road and turned into the woods.'

'It will only take a minute,' said Mityushin.

The three of them entered the tavern. A fat woman was wiping the counter with a rag. She scowled at them and poured three mugs of beer.

Anton Petrovich swallowed, choked slightly, and said, 'Excuse me for a second.'

'Hurry,' said Mityushin, putting his mug back on the bar.

Anton Petrovich turned into the passage, followed the arrow to men, mankind, human beings, marched past the toilet, past the kitchen, gave a start when a cat darted under his feet, quickened his step, reached the end of the passage, pushed open a door, and a shower of sunlight splashed his face. He found himself in a little green yard, where hens walked about and a boy in a faded bathing suit sat on a log. Anton Petrovich rushed past him, past some elder bushes, down a couple of wooden steps and into more bushes, then suddenly slipped, for the ground sloped. Branches whipped against his face, and he pushed them aside awkwardly, diving and slipping; the slope, overgrown with elder, kept growing steeper. At last his headlong descent became uncontrollable. He slid down on tense, outspread legs, warding off the springy twigs. Then he embraced an unexpected tree at full speed, and began moving obliquely. The bushes thinned out. Ahead was a tall fence. He saw a loophole in it, rustled through the nettles, and found himself in a pine grove, where shadow-dappled laundry hung between the tree trunks near a shack. With the same purposefulness he traversed the grove and presently realized that he was again sliding downhill. Ahead of him water shimmered among the trees. He stumbled, then saw a path to his right. It led him to the lake.

An old fisherman, suntanned, the color of smoked flounder and wearing a straw hat, indicated the way to the Wannsee station. The road at first skirted the lake, then turned into the forest, and he wandered through the woods for about two hours before emerging at the railroad tracks. He trudged to the nearest station, and as he reached it a train approached. He boarded a car and squeezed in between two passengers, who glanced with curiosity at this fat, pale, moist man in black, with painted cheeks and dirty shoes, a monocle in his begrimed eye socket. Only upon reaching Berlin, did he pause for a moment, or at least he had the sensation that, up to that moment, he had been fleeing continuously and only now had stopped to catch his breath and look around him. He was in a familiar square. Beside him an old flower woman with an enormous woollen bosom was selling carnations. A man in an armor-like coating of newspapers was touting the title of a local scandal sheet. A shoe-shine man gave Anton Petrovich a fawning look. Anton Petrovich sighed with relief and placed his foot firmly on the stand; whereupon the man's elbows began working lickety-split.

'It is all horrible, of course,' he thought, as he watched the tip of his shoe begin to gleam. 'But I am alive, and for the moment that is the main thing.' Mityushin and Gnuschke had probably traveled back to town and were standing guard before his house, so he would have to wait a while for things to blow over. In no circumstances must he meet them. Much later he would go to fetch his things. And he must leave Berlin that very night. . . .

'*Dobryy den*' (Good day), Anton Petrovich,' came a gentle voice right above his ear.

He gave such a start that his foot slipped off the stand. No, it was all right—false alarm. The voice belonged to a certain Leontiev, a man he had met three or four times, a journalist or something of the sort. A talkative, but harmless fellow. They said his wife deceived him right and left.

'Out for a stroll?' asked Leontiev, giving him a melancholy handshake.

'Yes. No, I have various things to do,' replied Anton Petrovich, thinking at the same time: 'I hope he proceeds on his way, otherwise it will be quite dreadful.'

Leontiev looked around, and said, as if he had made a happy discovery, 'Splendid weather!'

Actually he was a pessimist and, like all pessimists, a ridiculously unobservant man. His face was ill-shaven, yellowish and long, and all of him looked clumsy, emaciated, and lugubrious, as if nature had suffered from toothache when creating him.

The shoeshine man jauntily clapped his brushes together. Anton Petrovich looked at his revived shoes.

'Which way are you headed?' asked Leontiev.

'And you?' asked Anton Petrovich.

'Makes no difference to me. I'm free right now. I can keep you company for a while.' He cleared his throat and added insinuatingly, 'If you allow me, of course.'

'Of course, please do,' mumbled Anton Petrovich. Now he's attached himself, he thought. Must find some less familiar street, or else more acquaintances will turn up. If I can only avoid meeting those two. . . .

'Well, how is life treating you?' asked Leontiev. He belonged to the breed of people who ask how life is treating you only to give a detailed account of how it is treating them.

'Oh, well, I am all right,' Anton Petrovich replied. Of course he'll find out all about it afterwards. Good Lord, what a mess. 'I am going this way,' he said aloud, and turned sharply. Smiling sadly at his own thoughts, Leontiev almost ran into him and swayed slightly on lanky legs. 'This way? All right, it's all the same to me.'

'What shall I do?' thought Anton Petrovich. 'After all, I can't just keep strolling with him like this. I have to think things over and decide so much. . . . And I'm awfully tired, and my corns hurt.'

As for Leontiev, he had already launched into a long story. He spoke in a level, unhurried voice. He spoke of how much he paid for his room, how hard it was to pay, how hard life was for him and his wife, how rarely one got a good landlady, how insolent theirs was with his wife.

'Adelaida Albertovna, of course, has a quick temper herself,' he added with a sigh. He was one of those middle-class Russians who use the patronymic when speaking of their spouses.

They were walking along an anonymous street, where the pavement was being repaired. One of the workmen had a dragon tattooed on his bare chest. Anton Petrovich wiped his forehead with his handkerchief and said:

'I have some business near here. They are waiting for me. A business appointment.'

'Oh, I'll walk you there,' said Leontiev sadly.

Anton Petrovich surveyed the street. A sign said 'Hotel.' A squalid and squat little hotel between a scaffolded building and a warehouse.

'I have to go in here,' said Anton Petrovich. 'Yes, this hotel. A business appointment.'

Leontiev took off his torn glove and gave him a soft handshake. 'Know what? I think I'll wait a while for you. Won't be long, will you?'

'Quite long, I'm afraid,' said Anton Petrovich.

'Pity. You see, I wanted to talk something over with you, and ask your advice. Well, no matter. I'll wait around for a while, just in case. Maybe you'll get through early.'

Anton Petrovich went into the hotel. He had no choice. It was empty and darkish inside. A disheveled person materialized from behind a desk and asked what he wanted.

'A room,' Anton Petrovich answered softly.

The man pondered this, scratched his head, and demanded a deposit. Anton Petrovich handed over ten marks. A red-haired maid, rapidly wiggling her behind, led him down a long corridor and unlocked a door. He entered, heaved a deep sigh, and sat down in a low armchair of ribbed velvet. He was alone. The furniture, the bed, the washstand seemed to awake, to give him a frowning look, and go back to sleep. In this drowsy, totally unremarkable hotel room, Anton Petrovich was at last alone.

Hunching over, covering his eyes with his hand, he lapsed into thought, and before him bright, speckled images passed by, patches of sunny greenery, a boy on the log, a fisherman, Leontiev, Berg, Tanya. And, at the thought of Tanya, he moaned and hunched over even more tensely. Her voice, her dear voice. So light, so girlish, quick of eye and limb, she would perch on the sofa, tuck her legs under her, and her skirt would float up around her like a silk dome and then drop back. Or else, she would sit at the table, quite motionless, only blinking now and then, and blowing out cigarette smoke with her face upturned. It's senseless.... Why did you cheat? For you did cheat. What shall I do without you? Tanya! ... Don't you see—you cheated. My darling— why? Why?

Emitting little moans and cracking his finger joints, he began pacing up and down the room, bumping against the furniture without noticing it. He happened to stop by the window and glance out into the street. At first he could not see the street because of the mist in his eyes, but presently the street appeared, with a truck at the curb, a bicyclist, an old lady gingerly stepping off the sidewalk. And along the sidewalk slowly strolled Leontiev, reading a newspaper as he went; he passed and turned the corner. And, for some reason, at the sight of Leontiev, Anton Petrovich realized just how hopeless his situation was—yes, hopeless, for there was no other word for it. Only yesterday he had been a perfectly honorable man, respected by friends, acquaintances, and fellow workers at the bank. His job! There was not even any question of it. Everything was different now: he had run down a slippery slope, and now he was at the bottom.

'But how can it be? I must decide to do something,' Anton Petrovich said in a thin voice. Perhaps there was a way out? They had tormented him for a while, but enough was enough. Yes, he had to decide. He remembered the suspicious gaze of the man at the desk. What should one say to that person? Oh, obviously: 'I'm going to fetch my luggage—I left it at the station.' So. Goodbye for ever, little hotel! The street, thank God, was now clear: Leontiev had finally given up and left. How do I get to the nearest streetcar stop? Oh, just go straight, my dear sir, and you will reach the nearest streetcar stop. No, better take a taxi. Off we go. The streets grow familiar again. Calmly, quite calmly. Tip the taxi driver. Home! Five floors. Calmly, quite calmly he went into the front hall. Then quickly opened the parlor door. My, what a surprise!

In the parlor, around the circular table, sat Mityushin, Gnuschke, and Tanya. On the table, stood bottles, glasses, and cups. Mityushin beamed—pink-faced, shiny-eyed, drunk as an owl. Gnuschke was drunk too, and also beamed, rubbing his hands together. Tanya was sitting with her bare elbows on the table, gazing at him motionlessly....

'At last!' exclaimed Mityushin, and took him by the arm. 'At last you've shown up!' He added in a whisper, with a mischievous wink, 'You, sly-boots, you!'

Anton Petrovich now sits down and has some vodka. Mityushin and Gnuschke keep giving him the same mischievous, but good-natured looks, Tanya says:

'You must be hungry. I'll get you a sandwich.'

Yes, a big ham sandwich, with the edge of fat overlapping. She goes to make it and then Mityushin and Gnuschke rush to him and begin to talk, interrupting each other.

'You lucky fellow! Just imagine—Mr. Berg also lost his nerve. Well, no "also," but, lost his nerve anyhow. While we were waiting for you at the tavern, his seconds came in and announced that Berg had changed his mind. Those broad-shouldered bullies always turn out to be cowards. "Gentlemen, we ask you to excuse us for having agreed to act as seconds for this scoundrel." That's how lucky you are, Anton Petrovich! So everything is now just dandy. And you came out of it honorably, while he is disgraced forever. And, most important, your wife, when she heard about it, immediately left Berg and returned to you. And you must forgive her.'

Anton Petrovich smiled broadly, got up, and started fiddling with the ribbon of his monocle. His smile slowly faded away. Such things don't happen in real life.

He looked at the moth-eaten plush, the plump bed, the washstand, and this wretched room in this wretched hotel seemed to him to be the room in which he would have to live from that day on. He sat down on the bed, took off his shoes, wiggled his toes with relief, and noticed that there was a blister on his heel, and a corresponding hole in his sock. Then he rang the bell and ordered a ham sandwich. When the maid placed the plate on the table, he deliberately looked away but as soon as the door had shut, he grabbed the sandwich with both hands, immediately soiled his fingers and chin with the hanging margin of fat, and, grunting greedily, began to munch.

Berlin, 1927

LIK

There is a play of the nineteen-twenties, called *L'Abîme* (*'The Abyss'*), by the well-known French author Suire. It has already passed from the stage straight into the Lesser Lethe (the one, that is, that serves the theater—a stream, incidentally, not quite as hopeless as the main river, and containing a weaker solution of oblivion, so that angling producers may still fish something out many years later). This play—essentially idiotic, even ideally idiotic, or, putting it another way, ideally constructed on the solid conventions of traditional dramaturgy—deals with the torments of a middle-aged, rich, and religious French lady suddenly inflamed by a sinful passion for a young Russian named Igor, who has turned up at her château and fallen in love with her daughter Angélique. An old friend of the family, a strong-willed, sullen bigot, conveniently knocked together by the author out of mysticism and lechery, is jealous of the heroine's interest in Igor, while she in turn is jealous of the latter's attentions to Angélique, in a word, it is all very compelling and true to life, every speech bears the trade mark of a respectable tradition, and it goes without saying that there is not a single jolt of talent to disrupt the ordered course of action, swelling where it ought to swell, and interrupted when necessary by a lyric scene or a shamelessly explanatory dialogue between two old retainers.

The apple of discord is usually an early, sour fruit, and should be cooked. Thus the young man of the play threatens to be somewhat colorless, and it is in a vain attempt to touch him up a little that the author has made him a Russian, with all the obvious consequences of

53

such trickery. According to Suire's optimistic intention, he is an émigré Russian aristocrat, recently adopted by an old lady, the Russian wife of a neighboring land-owner. One night, at the height of a thunderstorm, Igor comes knocking at our door, enters, riding crop in hand, and announces in agitation that the pinewood is burning on his benefactress's estate, and that our pinery is also in danger. This affects us less strongly than the visitor's youthful glamour, and we are inclined to sink onto a hassock, toying pensively with our necklace, whereupon our bigot friend observes that the reflection of flames is at times more dangerous than the conflagration itself. . . . A solid, high-quality plot, as you can see, for it is clear at once that the Russian will become a regular caller and, in fact, Act Two is all sunny weather and bright summer clothes.

Judging by the printed text of the play, Igor expresses himself (at least in the first scenes, before the author tires of this) not inncorrectly but, as it were, a bit hesitantly, every so often interposing a questioning 'I think that is how you say it in French?' Later, though, when the turbulent flow of the drama leaves the author no time for such trifles, all foreign peculiarities of speech are dis-carded and the young Russian spontaneously acquires the rich vocabulary of a native Frenchman; it is only toward the end, during the lull before the final burst of action, that the playwright remembers with a start the nationality of Igor, whereupon the latter casually addresses these words to the old manservant: '*J'étais trop jeune pour prendre part à la . . . comment dit-on . . . velika voïna . . . grande, grande guerre. . . .*' In all fairness to the author, it is true that, except for this '*velika voïna*' and one modest '*dosvidania*,' he does not abuse his acquaintance with the Russian language, contenting himself with the stage direction 'Slavic singsong lends a certain charm to Igor's speech.'

In Paris, where the play had great success, Igor was played by François Coulot, and played not badly but for some reason with a strong Italian accent, which he evidently wanted to pass off as Russian, and which did not surprise a single Parisian critic. Afterwards, when the play trickled down into the provinces, this role fell by chance to a real Russian actor, Lik (stage name of Lavrentiy Ivanovich Kruzhevnitsyn), a lean, fair-haired fellow with coffee-dark eyes, who had previously won some fame, thanks to a film in which he did an excellent job in the bit part of a stutterer.

It was hard to say, though, if Lik (the word means 'appearance' in Russian and Middle English) possessed genuine theatrical talent or was a man of many indistinct callings who had chosen one of them at random but could just as well have been a painter, jeweler, or rat-catcher. Such a person resembles a room with a number of different doors, among which there is perhaps one that does lead straight into some great garden, into the moon-lit depths of a marvelous human night, where the soul discovers the treasure intended for it alone. But, be that as it may, Lik had failed to open *that* door, taking instead the Thespian path, which he followed without enthusiasm, with the absent manner of a man looking for signposts that do not exist but that perhaps have appeared to him in a dream, or can be distinguished in the undeveloped photograph of some other locality that he will never, never visit. On the conventional plane of earthly habitus, he was in his thirties, and so was the century. In elderly people stranded not only outside the border of their country but outside that of their own lives, nostalgia evolves into an extraordinarily complex organ, which functions continuously, and its secretion compensates for all that has been lost; or else it becomes a fatal tumor on the soul that makes it painful to breathe, sleep, and associate with carefree foreigners. In Lik, this memory of Russia remained in the embryonic state, confined to misty childhood recollections, such as the resinous fragrance of the first spring day in the country, or the special shape of the snowflake on the wool of his hood. His parents were dead. He lived alone. There was always something sleazy about the loves and friendships that came his way. Nobody wrote gossipy letters to him, nobody took a greater interest in his worries than he did himself, and there was no one to go and complain to about the undeserved precariousness of his very being when he learned from two doctors, a Frenchman and a Russian, that (like many protagonists) he had an incurable heart ailment—while the streets were virtually swarming with robust oldsters. There seemed to be a certain connection between this illness of his and his fondness for fine, expensive things; he might, for example, spend his last 200 francs on a scarf or a fountain pen, but it always, always happened that the scarf would soon get soiled, the pen broken, despite the meticulous, even pious, care he took of things.

In relation to the other members of the company, which he had joined as casually as a fur doffed by a woman lands on this or that quite anonymous chair, he remained as much a stranger as he had been at the first rehearsal. He had immediately had the feeling of being superfluous, of having usurped someone else's place. The director of the company was invariably friendly toward him, but Lik's hypersensitive soul constantly imagined the possibility of a row—as if at any moment he might be unmasked and accused of something unbearably shameful. The very constancy of the director's attitude he interpreted as the utmost indifference to his work, as though everyone had long since reconciled himself to its hopelessly poor quality—and he was being tolerated merely because there was no convenient pretext for his dismissal.

It seemed to him—and perhaps this was actually so—that to these loud, sleek French actors, interconnected by a network of personal and professional passions, he was as much a chance object as the old bicycle that one of the characters deftly disassembled in the second act; hence, when someone gave him a particularly hearty greeting or offered him a cigarette, he would think that there was some misunderstanding, which would, alas, be resolved in a moment. Because of his illness he avoided drinking, but his absence from friendly gatherings, instead of being attributed to lack of sociability (leading to accusations of haughtiness and thus endowing him with, at least, some semblance of a personality), simply went unnoticed, as if there was no question of its being otherwise; and if they did happen to invite him somewhere, it was always in a vaguely interrogative manner ('Coming with us, or . . . ?')—a manner particularly painful to one who is yearning to be persuaded to come. He understood little of the jokes, allusions, and nicknames that the other bandied about with cryptic gaiety. He almost wished some of the joking were at his expense, but even this failed to happen. At the same time, he rather liked some of his colleagues. The actor who played the bigot was in real life a pleasant fat fellow, who had recently purchased a sports car, about which he would talk to you with genuine inspiration. And the ingénue was most charming, too—dark-haired and slender, with her splendidly bright, carefully made-up eyes—but in daytime hopelessly oblivious of her evening confessions on the stage, in the garrulous embrace of her Russian fiancé, to whom she so candidly clung. Lik liked to tell himself that only on the stage did she live her true life, being subject the rest of the time to periodic fits of insanity, during which she no longer recognized him and called herself by a different name. With the leading lady he never exchanged a single word apart from their lines, and when this thickset, tense, handsome woman walked past him in the wings, her jowls shaking, he had the feeling that he was but a piece of scenery, apt to fall flat on the floor if someone brushed against him. It is indeed difficult to say whether it was all as poor Lik imagined or whether these perfectly harmless, self-centered people left him alone simply because he did not seek their company, and did not start a conversation with him just as passengers who have established contact among themselves do not address the foreigner absorbed in his book in a corner of the compartment. But even if Lik did attempt in rare moments of self-confidence to convince himself of the irrationality of his vague torments, the memory of similar torments was too recent, and they were too often repeated in new circumstances, for him to be able to overcome them now. Loneliness as a situation can be corrected, but as a state of mind it is an incurable illness.

He played his part conscientiously, and, at least as far as accent was concerned, more successfully than his predecessor, since Lik spoke French with a Russian lilt, drawing out and softening his sentences, dropping the stress before their close, and filtering off with excessive care the spray of auxiliary expressions that so nimbly and rapidly fly off a Frenchman's tongue. His part was so small, so inconsequential, in spite of its dramatic impact on the actions of the other characters, that it was not worth pondering over; yet he would ponder, especially at the outset of the tour, and not so much out of love for his art as because the disparity between the insignificance of the role itself and the importance of the complex drama of which he was the prime cause struck him as being a paradox that somehow humiliated him personally. However, although he soon cooled to the possibility of improvements suggested to him by both art and vanity (two things that often coincide), he would hurry on-stage with unchanged, mysterious delight, as though, every time, he anticipated some special reward —in no way connected, of course, with the customary dose of neutral applause. Neither did this reward consist in the performer's inner satisfaction. Rather, it lurked in certain extraordinary furrows and folds that he discerned in the life of the play itself, banal and hopelessly pedestrian as it was, for, like any piece acted out by live people, it gained, God knows whence, an individual soul, and attempted for a couple of hours to exist, to evolve its own heat and energy, bearing no relation to its author's pitiful conception or the mediocrity of the players, but awakening, as life awakes in water warmed by sunlight. For instance, Lik might hope one vague and lovely night, in the midst of the usual performance, to tread, as it were, on a quicksandy spot; something would give, and he would sink forever in a newborn element, unlike anything known—independently developing the play's threadbare themes in ways altogether new. He would pass irrevocably into this element, marry Angélique, go riding over the crisp heather, receive all the material wealth hinted at in the play, go to live in that castle, and, moreover, find himself in a world of ineffable tenderness—a bluish, delicate world where fabulous adventures of the senses occur, and unheard-of metamorphoses of the mind. As he thought about all this, Lik imagined for some reason that when he died of heart failure—and he would die soon—the attack would certainly come on-stage, as it had been with poor Molière, barking out his dog Latin among the doctors; but that he would not notice his death, crossing over instead into the actual world of a chance play, now blooming anew because of his arrival, while his smiling corpse lay on the boards, the toe of one foot protruding from beneath the folds of the lowered curtain.

At the end of the summer, *The Abyss* and two other plays in the repertory were running at a Mediterranean town. Lik appeared only in *The Abyss*, so between the first performance and the second (only two were scheduled) he had a week of free time, which he did not quite know how to use. What is more, the southern climate did not agree with him; he went through the first performance in a blur of greenhouse delirium, with a hot drop of greasepaint now hanging from the tip of his nose, now scalding his upper lip, and when, during the first intermission, he went out on the terrace separating the back of the theater from an Anglican church, he suddenly felt he would not last out the performance, but would dissolve on the stage amid many-colored exhalations, through which, at the final mortal instant, would flash the blissful ray of another—yes, another life. Nevertheless, he made it to the end somehow or other, even if he did see double from the sweat in his eyes, while the smooth contact of his young partner's cool bare arms agonizingly accentuated the melting state of his palms. He returned to his boardinghouse quite shattered, with aching shoulders and a reverberating pain in the back of his head. In the dark garden, everything was in bloom and smelled of candy, and there was a continuous trilling of crickets, which he mistook (as all Russians do) for cicadas.

His illuminated room was antiseptically white compared to the southern darkness framed in the open window. He crushed a red-bellied drunken mosquito on the wall, then sat for a long time on the edge of the bed, afraid to lie down, afraid of the palpitations. The proximity of the sea whose presence he divined beyond the lemon grove oppressed him, as if this ample, viscously glistening space, with only a membrane of moonlight stretched tight across its surface, was akin to the equally taut vessel of his drumming heart, and, like it, was agonizingly bare, with nothing to separate it from the sky, from the shuffling of human feet and the unbearable pressure of the music playing in a nearby bar. He glanced at the expensive watch on his wrist and noticed with a pang that he had lost the crystal; yes, his cuff had brushed against a stone parapet as he had stumbled uphill a while ago. The watch was still alive, defenseless and naked, like a live organ exposed by the surgeon's knife.

He passed his days in a quest for shade and a longing for coolness. There was something infernal in the glimpses of sea and beach, where bronzed demons basked on the torrid shingle. The sunny side of the narrow streets was so strictly forbidden to him that he would have had to solve intricate route-finding problems if there had been purpose in his wanderings. He had, however, nowhere to go. He strolled aimlessly along the shop fronts, which displayed, among other objects, some rather amusing bracelets of what looked like pink amber, as well as decidedly attractive leather bookmarks and wallets tooled with gilt. He would sink into a chair beneath the orange awning of a café, then go home and lie on his bed—stark naked, dreadfully thin and white— and think about the same things he thought about incessantly.

He reflected that he had been condemned to live on the outskirts of life, that it had always been thus and always would be, and that, therefore, if death did not present him with an exit into true reality, he would simply never come to know life. He also reflected that if his parents were alive instead of having died at the dawn of émigré existence, the fifteen years of his adult life might have passed in the warmth of a family; that, had his destiny been less mobile, he would have finished one of the three high schools he had happened to attend at random points of middle, median, mediocre Europe, and would now have a good, solid job among good, solid people. But, strain his imagination as he might, he could not picture either that job or those people, just as he could not explain to himself why he had studied as a youth at a screen-acting school, instead of taking up music or numismatics, window-washing, or bookkeeping. And, as always, from each point of its circumference his thought would follow a radius back to the dark center, to the presentiment of nearing death, for which he, who had accumulated no spiritual treasures, was hardly an interesting prey. Nonetheless, she had apparently determined to give him precedence.

One evening, as he was reclining in a canvas chair on the veranda, he was importuned by one of the pension guests, a loquacious old Russian (who had managed on two occasions already to recount to Lik the story of his life, first in one direction, from the present toward the past, and then in the other, against the grain, resulting in two different lives, one successful, the other not), who, settling himself comfortably and fingering his chin said: 'A friend of mine has turned up here; that is, a "friend," *c'est beaucoup dire*—I met him a couple of times in Brussels, that's all. Now, alas, he's a completely derelict character. Yesterday—yes, I think it was yesterday—I happened to mention your name, and he says, "Why, of course I know him—in fact, we're even relatives."'

'Relatives?' asked Lik with surprise. 'I almost never had any relatives. What's his name?'

'A certain Koldunov—Oleg Petrovich Koldunov.... Petrovich, isn't it? Know him?'

'It just can't be!' cried Lik, covering his face with his hands.

'Yes. Imagine!' said the other.

'It can't be,' repeated Lik. 'You see, I always thought——. This is awful! You didn't give him my address, did you?'

'I did. I understand, though. One feels disgusted and sorry at the same time. Kicked out of everywhere, embittered, has a family, and so on.'

'Listen, do me a favor. Can't you tell him I've left.'

'If I see him, I'll tell him. But . . . well, I just happened to run into him down at the port. My, what lovely yachts they have down there. That's what I call fortunate people. You live on the water, and sail wherever you feel like. Champagne, girlies, everything all polished. . . .'

And the old fellow smacked his lips and shook his head.

What a mad thing to happen, Lik thought all evening. What a mess. . . . He did not know what had given him the idea that Oleg Koldunov was no longer among the living. It was one of those axioms that the rational mind no longer keeps on active duty, relegating it to the remotest depths of consciousness, so that now, with Koldunov's resurrection, he had to admit the possibility of two parallel lines crossing after all; yet it was agonizingly difficult to get rid of the old concept, embedded in his brain—as if the extraction of this single false notion might vitiate the entire order of his other notions and concepts. And now he simply could not recall what data had led him to conclude that Koldunov had perished, and why, in the past twenty years, there had been such a strengthening in the chain of dim initial information out of which Koldunov's doom had been wrought.

Their mothers had been cousins. Oleg Koldunov was

two years his elder; for four years they had gone to the same provincial high school, and the memory of these years had always been so hateful to Lik that he preferred not to recall his boyhood. Indeed, his Russia was perhaps so thickly clouded over for the very reason that he did not cherish any personal recollections. Dreams, however, would still occur even now, for there was no control over them. Sometimes Koldunov would appear in person, in his own image, in the surroundings of boyhood, hastily assembled by the director of dreams out of such accessories as a classroom, desks, a blackboard, and its dry, weightless sponge. Besides these down-to-earth dreams there were also romantic, even decadent ones—devoid, that is, of Koldunov's obvious presence but coded by him, saturated with his oppressive spirit or filled with rumors about him, with situations and shadows of situations somehow expressing his essence. And this excruciating Koldunovian décor, against which the action of a chance dream would develop, was far worse than the straightforward dream visitations of Koldunov as Lik remembered him—a coarse, muscular high-school boy, with cropped hair and a disagreeably handsome face. The regularity of his strong features was spoiled by eyes that were set too close together and equipped with heavy, leathery lids (no wonder they had dubbed him 'The Crocodile,' for indeed there was a certain turbid muddy-Nile quality in his glance).

Koldunov had been a hopelessly poor student; his was that peculiarly Russian hopelessness of the seemingly bewitched dunce as he sinks, in a vertical position, through the transparent strata of several repeated classes, so that the youngest boys gradually reach his level, numb with fear, and then, a year later, leave him behind with relief. Koldunov was remarkable for his insolence, uncleanliness, and savage physical strength; after one had a tussle with him, the room would always reek of the menagerie. Lik, on the other hand, was a frail, sensitive, vulnerably proud boy, and therefore represented an ideal, inexhaustible prey. Koldunov would come flowing over him wordlessly, and industriously torture the squashed but always squirming victim on the floor. Koldunov's enormous, splayed palm would go into an obscene, scooping motion as it penetrated the convulsive, panic-stricken depths it sought. Thereupon he would leave Lik, whose back was covered with chalk dust and whose tormented ears were aflame, in peace for an hour or two, content to repeat some obscenely meaningless phrase, insulting to Lik. Then, when the urge returned, Koldunov would sigh, almost reluctantly, before piling on him again, digging his hornlike nails into Lik's ribs or sitting down for a rest on the victim's face. He had a thorough knowledge of all the bully's devices for causing the sharpest pain without leaving marks, and therefore enjoyed the servile respect of his schoolmates. At the same time he nurtured a vaguely sentimental affection for his habitual patient, making a point of strolling with his arm around the other's shoulders during the class breaks, his heavy, distrait paw palpating the thin collarbone, while Lik tried in vain to preserve an air of independence and dignity. Thus Lik's school days were an utterly absurd and unbearable torment. He was embarrassed to complain to anyone, and his nighttime thoughts of how he would finally kill Koldunov merely drained his spirit of all strength. Fortunately, they almost never met outside of school, although Lik's mother would have liked to establish closer ties with her cousin, who was much richer than she and kept her own horses. Then the Revolution began rearranging the furniture, and Lik found himself in a different city, while fifteen-year-old Oleg, already sporting a mustache and completely brutified, disappeared in the general confusion, and a blissful lull began. It was soon replaced, however, by new, more subtle tortures at the hands of the intial rackmaster's minor successors.

Sad to say, on the rare occasions when Lik spoke of his past, he would publicly recall the presumed deceased with that artificial smile with which we reward a distant time ('Those were the happy days') that sleeps with a full belly in a corner of its evil-smelling cage. Now, however, when Koldunov proved to be alive, no matter what adult arguments Lik invoked, he could not conquer the same sensation of helplessness—metamorphosed by reality but all the more manifest—that oppressed him in dreams when from behind a curtain, smirking, fiddling with his belt buckle, stepped the lord of the dream, a dark, dreadful schoolboy. And, even though Lik understood perfectly well that the real, live Koldunov would not harm him now, the possibility of meeting him seemed ominous, fateful, dimly linked to the whole system of evil, with its premonitions of torment and abuse, so familiar to him.

After his conversation with the old man, Lik decided to stay at home as little as possible. Only three days remained before the last performance, so it was not worth the trouble to move to a different boarding house; but he could, for instance, take daylong trips across the

Italian border or into the mountains, since the weather had grown much cooler, with a drizzling rain and a brisk wind. Early next morning, walking along a narrow path between flower-hung walls, he saw coming toward him a short, husky man, whose dress in itself differed little from the usual uniform of the Mediterranean vacationer —beret, open-necked shirt, espadrilles—but somehow suggested not so much the license of the season as the compulsion of poverty. In the first instant, Lik was struck most of all by the fact that the monstrous figure that filled his memory with its bulk proved to be in reality hardly taller than himself.

'Lavrentiy, Lavrusha, don't you recognize me?' Koldunov drawled dramatically, stopping in the middle of the path.

The large features of that sallow face with a rough shadow on its cheeks and upper lip, that glimpse of bad teeth, that large, insolent Roman nose, that bleary, questioning gaze—all of it was Koldunovian, indisputably so, even if dimmed by time. But, as Lik looked, this resemblance noiselessly disintegrated, and before him stood a disreputable stranger with the massive face of a Caesar, though a very shabby one.

'Let's kiss like good Russians,' Koldunov said grimly, and pressed his cold, salty cheek for an instant against Lik's childish lips.

'I recognized you immediately,' babbled Lik. 'Just yesterday I heard about you from What's-His-Name ... Gavrilyuk.'

'Dubious character,' interrupted Koldunov. '*Méfie-toi*. Well, well—so here is my Lavrusha. Remarkable! I'm glad. Glad to meet you again. That's fate for you! Remember, Lavrusha, how we used to catch gobies together? As clear as if it happened yesterday. One of my fondest memories. Yes.'

Lik knew perfectly well that he had never fished with Koldunov, but confusion, ennui, and timidity prevented him from accusing this stranger of appropriating a nonexistent past. He suddenly felt wiggly and overdressed.

'How many times,' continued Koldunov, examining with interest Lik's pale-gray trousers, 'how many times during the past years.... Oh yes, I thought of you. Yes, indeed! And where, thought I, is my Lavrusha? I've told my wife about you. She was once a pretty woman. And what line of work are you in?'

'I'm an actor,' sighed Lik.

'Allow me an indiscretion,' said Koldunov in a confidential tone. 'I'm told that in the United States there is a secret society that considers the word "money" improper, and if payment must be made, they wrap the dollars in toilet paper. True, only the rich belong—the poor have no time for it. Now, here's what I'm driving at,' and, his brows raised questioningly, Koldunov made a vulgar, palpating motion with two fingers and thumb —the feel of hard cash.

'Alas, no!' Lik exclaimed innocently. 'Most of the year I'm unemployed, and the pay is miserable.'

'I know how it is and understand perfectly,' said Koldunov with a smile. 'In any case.... Oh, yes—in any case, there's a project I'd like to discuss with you sometime. You could make a nice little profit. Are you doing anything right now?'

'Well, you see, as a matter of fact, I'm going to Bordighera for the whole day, by bus.... And tomorrow....'

'What a shame—if you had told me, there's a Russian chauffeur I know here, with a smart private car, and I would have shown you the whole Riviera. You ninny! All right, all right, I'll walk you to the bus stop.'

'And anyway I'm leaving for good soon,' Lik put in.

'Tell me, how's the family? ... How's Aunt Natasha?' Koldunov asked absently as they walked along a crowded little street that led down to the seafront. 'I see, I see,' he nodded at Lik's reply. Suddenly a guilty, demented look passed fleetingly across his evil face. 'Listen, Lavrusha,' he said, pushing him involuntarily and bringing his face close to Lik's on the narrow sidewalk. 'Meeting you is an omen for me. It is a sign that all is not lost yet, and I must admit that just the other day I was thinking that all *was* lost. Do you understand what I am saying?'

'Oh, everybody has such thoughts now and then,' said Lik.

They reached the promenade. The sea was opaque and corrugated under the overcast sky, and, here and there near the parapet the foam had splashed onto the pavement. There was no one about except for a solitary lady in slacks sitting on a bench with an open book in her lap.

'Here, give me five francs and I'll buy you some cigarettes for the trip,' Koldunov said rapidly. Taking the money, he added in a different, easy tone, 'Look, that's the little wife over there—keep her company for a minute, and I'll be right back.'

Lik went up to the blond lady and said with an actor's automatism, 'Your husband will be right back and forgot to introduce me. I'm a cousin of his.'

70

At the same moment he was sprinkled by the cool
dust of a breaker. The lady looked up at Lik with blue,
English eyes, unhurriedly closed her red book, and left
without a word.

'Just a joke,' said Koldunov, as he reappeared, out of
breath. '*Voilà*. I'll take a few for myself. Yes, I'm afraid
my little woman has no time to sit on a bench and look
at the sea. I implore you, promise me that we'll meet
again. Remember the omen! Tomorrow, after tomorrow, whenever you want. Promise me! Wait, I'll give
you my address.'

He took Lik's brand-new gilt-and-leather notebook, sat
down, bent forward his sweaty, swollen-veined forehead, joined his knees, and not only wrote his address,
reading it over with agonizing care, redotting an 'i' and
underlining a word, but also sketched a street map: so,
so, then so. Evidently he had done this more than once,
and more than once people had stood him up, using the
forgotten address as an excuse; hence he wrote with great
diligence and force—a force that was almost incanta-
tional.

The bus arrived. 'So, I'll expect you!' shouted Koldunov, helping Lik aboard. Then he turned, full of
energy and hope, and walked resolutely off along the
promenade as if he had some pressing, important business, though it was perfectly obvious that he was an
idler, a drunkard, and a boor.

The following day, a Wednesday, Lik took a trip to
the mountains, and then spent the greater part of Thurs-
day lying in his room with a bad headache. The performance was that evening, the departure tomorrow. At
about six in the afternoon, he went out to pick up his

watch at the jeweler's and buy some nice white shoes—
an innovation he had long wanted to sport in the second
act. Separating the lead curtain, he emerged from the
shop, shoebox under arm, and ran straight into Koldunov.

Koldunov's greeting lacked the former ardor, and had
a slightly derisive note instead. 'Oho! You won't wriggle
out of it this time,' he said, taking Lik firmly by the
elbow. 'Come on, let's go. You'll see how I live and
work.'

'I have a performance tonight,' Lik objected, 'and I'm
leaving tomorrow!'

'That's just the point, my friend, that's just the point.
Seize the opportunity! Take advantage of it! There will
never be another chance. The card is trumped! Come
on. Get going.'

Repeating disconnected words and imitating with all
his unattractive being the senseless joy of a man who has
reached the borderline, and perhaps even gone beyond it
(a poor imitation, Lik thought vaguely), Koldunov
walked briskly, prodding on his weak companion. The
entire company of actors was sitting on the terrace of a
corner café, and, noticing Lik, greeted him with a peri-
patetic smile that really did not belong to any one mem-
ber of the group, but skittered across the lips of each like
an independent spot of reflected sunlight.

Koldunov led Lik up a crooked little street, mottled
here and there by jaundiced crooked, sunlight. Lik had
never visited this squalid, old quarter. The tall, bare
façades of the narrow houses seemed to lean over the
pavement from either side, with their tops almost meeting; sometimes they coalesced completely, forming an

arch. Repulsive infants were puttering about by the doorways; black, foul-smelling water ran down the sidewalk gutter. Suddenly changing direction, Koldunov shoved him into a shop and, flaunting the cheapest French slang (in the manner of many Russian paupers), bought two bottles of wine with Lik's money. It was evident that he was long since in debt here, and now there was a desperate glee in his whole bearing and in his menacing exclamations of greeting, which brought no response whatever from either the shopkeeper or the shopkeeper's mother-in-law, and this made Lik even more uncomfortable. They walked on, turning into an alley, and although it had seemed that the vile street they had just ascended represented the utmost limit of squalor, filth, and congestion, this passage, with limp washing hanging overhead, managed to embody an even greater dejection. At the corner of a lopsided little square, Koldunov said that he would go in first, and, leaving Lik, headed for the black cavity of an open door. Simultaneously a fair-haired little boy came dashing out of it, but, seeing the advancing Koldunov, ran back, brushing against a pail which reacted with a harsh clink. 'Wait, Vasyuk!' shouted Koldunov, and lumbered into his murky abode. As soon as he entered, a frenzied female voice issued from within, yelling something in what seemed a habitually overwrought tone, but then the scream ceased abruptly, and a minute later Koldunov peeped out and grimly beckoned to Lik.

Lik crossed the threshold and immediately found himself in a low-ceilinged, dark room, whose bare walls, as if distorted by some awful pressure from above, formed incomprehensible curves and corners. The place was

crammed with the dingy stage properties of indigence.
The boy of a moment ago sat on the sagging connubial
bed; a huge fair-haired woman with thick bare feet
emerged from a corner and, without a smile on her
bloated pale face (whose every feature, even the eyes,
seemed smudged, by fatigue, or melancholy, or God
knows what), wordlessly greeted Lik.

'Get acquainted, get acquainted,' Koldunov muttered
in derisive encouragement, and immediately set about
uncorking the wine. His wife put some bread and a plate
of tomatoes on the table. She was so silent that Lik began to doubt whether it had been this woman who had
screamed a moment ago.

She sat down on a bench in the back of the room,
busying herself with something, cleaning something ...
with a knife over a spread newspaper, it seemed—Lik
was afraid to look too closely—while the boy, his eyes
glistening, moved over to the wall and, maneuvering
cautiously, slipped out into the street. There was a multi-
tude of flies in the room, and with maniacal pesistence
they haunted the table and settled on Lik's forehead.

'All right, let's have a drink,' said Koldunov.

'I can't—I'm not allowed to,' Lik was about to object,
but instead, obeying the oppressive influence he knew
well from his nightmares, he took a swallow—and went
into a fit of coughing.

'That's better,' said Koldunov with a sigh, wiping his
trembling lips with the back of his hand. 'You see,' he
continued, filling Lik's glass and his own, 'here's the
situation. This is going to be a business talk! Allow me
to tell you in brief. At the beginning of summer, I
worked for a month or so with some other Russians

here, collecting beach garbage. But, as you well know, I am an outspoken man who likes the truth, and when a scoundrel turns up, I come right out and say, "You're a scoundrel," and, if necessary, I punch him in the mouth. Well, one day . . .'

And Koldunov began telling, circumstantially, with painstaking repetitions, a dull, wretched episode, and one had the feeling that for a long time his life had consisted of such episodes; that humiliation and failure, heavy cycles of ignoble idleness and ignoble toil, culminating in the inevitable row, had long since become a profession with him. Lik, meanwhile, began to feel drunk after the first glass, but nevertheless went on sipping, with concealed revulsion. A kind of tickling fog permeated every part of his body, but he dared not stop, as if his refusal of wine would lead to a shameful punishment. Leaning on one elbow, Koldunov talked uninterruptedly, stroking the edge of the table with one hand and occasionally slapping it to stress some particularly somber word. His head, the color of yellowish clay (he was almost completely bald), the bags under his eyes, the enigmatically malignant expression of his mobile nostrils —all of this had completely lost any connection with the image of the strong, handsome schoolboy who used to torment Lik, but the coefficient of nightmare remained unchanged.

'There you are, friend. . . . This is no longer important,' said Koldunov in a different, less narrative tone. 'Actually, I had this little tale all ready for you last time, when it occurred to me that fate—I'm an old fatalist— had given a certain meaning to our meeting, that you had come as a savior, so to speak. But now it turns out that, in the first place, you—forgive me—are as stingy as a Jew and, in the second place.... Who knows, maybe you really are not in a position to make me a loan.... Have no fear, have no fear.... This topic is closed! Moreover, it would have only been a question of a small-sum to get me back not on my feet—that would be a luxury—but merely on all fours. Because I'm sick of sprawling with my face in the muck. I'm not going to ask anything of you; it's not my style to beg. All I want is your opinion, about something. It's merely a philosophi-cal question. Ladies need not listen. How do you explain all this? You see, if a definite explanation exists, then fine, I'm willing to put up with the muck, since that means there is something logical and justified in all this, perhaps something useful to me or to others, I don't know. Here, explain this to me: I am a human being—you certainly cannot deny that, can you? All right. I am a human being, and the same blood runs in my veins as in yours. Believe it or not, I was my late mama's only and beloved. As a boy, I played pranks; as a youth, I went to war, and the ball started rolling—God, how it rolled! What went wrong? No, you tell *me*—what went wrong? I just want to know what went wrong, then I'll be satisfied. Why has life systematically baited me? Why have I been assigned the part of some kind of miserable scoundrel who is spat on by everybody, gypped, bullied, thrown into jail? Here's an example for you: When they were taking me away after a certain incident in Lyon—and I might add that I was absolutely in the right, and am now very sorry I did not finish him off—well, as the police was taking me away, ignoring my protests, you know what they did? They stuck a little hook right here in the live flesh of my neck—what kind of treatment is that, I ask you?—and off the cop led me to the police station, and I floated along like a sleepwalker, because every additional motion made me black out with pain. Well, can you explain why they don't do this to other people and then, all of a sudden, do it to me? Why did my first wife run away with a Circassian? Why did seven people nearly beat me to death in Antwerp in '32, in a small room? And look at all this—what's the reason for it?—these rags, these walls, that Katya over there? ... The story of my life interests me, and has so for a long while! This isn't any Jack London or Dostoyevski story for you! I live in a corrupt country—all right. I am willing to put up with the French. All right! But we must find some explanation, gentlemen! I was talking with a guy once, and he asks me, "Why don't you go back to Russia?" Why not, after all? The difference is very small! There they'd persecute me just the same, knock my teeth in, stick me in the cooler, and then invite me to be shot—and at least that would be honest. You see, I'm even willing to respect them—God knows, they are honest murderers—while here these crooks will think up such tortures for you, it's almost enough to make you feel nostalgic for the good old Russian bullet. Hey, why aren't you looking at me ... you, you, you ... or don't you understand what I'm saying?'

'No, I understand everything,' said Lik. 'Only please excuse me. I don't feel well, I must be going. I have to be at the theater soon.'

'Oh, no. Wait just a minute. I understand a few things myself. You're a strange fellow.... Come on, make me an offer of some kind.... Try! Maybe you'll shower me with gold after all, eh? Listen, you know what? I'll sell you a gun—it'll be very useful to you on the stage: bang, and down goes the hero. It's not even worth a hundred francs, but I need more than a hundred—I'll let you have it for a thousand. Want it?'

'No, I don't,' said Lik listlessly. 'And I really have no money. I've been through it all myself, the hunger and so forth.... No, I won't have any more, I feel sick.'

'You keep drinking, you son of a bitch, and you won't feel sick. All right, forget it. I just did it to see what you'd say—I won't be bought anyway. Only, please answer my question. Who was it decided I should suffer, and then condemned my child to the same lousy Russian fate? Just a minute, though—suppose I, too, want to sit down in my dressing gown and listen to the radio? What went wrong, eh? Take you, for instance—what makes you better than me? You go swaggering around, living in hotels, smooching with actresses.... What's the reason for it? Come on, explain it to me.'

Lik said, 'I turned out to have—I happened to have.... Oh, I don't know ... a modest dramatic talent, I suppose you could say.'

'Talent?' shouted Koldunov. 'I'll show you talent! I'll show you such talent that you'll start cooking apple-sauce in your pants! You're a dirty rat, chum. That's your only talent. I must say that's a good one!' (Koldunov started shaking in very primitive mimicry of side-splitting laughter.) So, according to you, I'm the lowest, filthiest vermin and deserve my rotten end? Splendid, simply splendid. Everything is explained—eureka, eureka! The card is trumped, the nail is in, the beast is butchered!'

'Oleg Petrovich is upset—maybe you ought to be going now,' Koldunov's wife suddenly said from her corner, with a strong Estonian accent. There was not the least trace of emotion in her voice, causing her remark to sound wooden and senseless. Koldunov slowly turned in his chair, without altering the position of his hand, which lay as if lifeless on the table, and fixed his wife with an enraptured gaze.

'I am not detaining anyone,' he spoke softly and cheerfully. 'And I'll be thankful not to be detained by others. Or told what to do. So long, Mister,' he added, not looking at Lik, who for some reason found it necessary to say:

'I'll write from Paris, without fail. . . .'

'So he's going to write, is he?' said Koldunov softly, apparently still addressing his wife. With some trouble Lik extricated himself from the chair and started in her direction, but swerved and bumped into the bed.

'Go away, it's all right,' she said calmly, and then, with a polite smile, Lik stumbled out of the house.

His first sensation was one of relief. He had escaped from the orbit of that drunken, moralizing moron. Then came a mounting horror: he was sick to his stomach, and his arms and legs belonged to different people. How was he to perform that night? The worst of all, though, was that his whole body, which seemed to consist of ripples and dots, sensed the approach of a heart attack. It was as if an invisible stake were pointing at him and he might impale himself any moment. This was why he must follow a weaving course, even stopping and backing slightly now and then. Nevertheless, his mind remained rather lucid; he knew that only thirty-six minutes remained before the start of the performance, and he knew the way home. . . . It would be a better idea, though, to go down to the embankment, to sit by the sea until he felt better. This will pass, this will pass, if only I don't die. . . . He also grasped the fact that the sun had just set, that the sky was already more luminous and more tender than the earth. What unnecessary, offensive nonsense. He walked, calculating every step, but sometimes he would err and passersby would turn to look at him. Happily, he did not encounter many of them, since it was the hallowed dinner hour, and when he reached the seafront, he found it quite deserted; the lights burned on the pier, casting long reflections on the tinted water, and these bright dots and inverted exclamation marks seemed to be shining translucently in his own head. He sat down on a bench, hurting his coccyx as he did so, and shut his eyes. But then everything began to spin; his heart was reflected as a terrifying globe on the dark inner-side of his eyelids. It continued to swell agonizingly, and, to put a stop to this, he opened his eyes and tried to hook his gaze on things—on the evening star, on that black buoy in the sea, on a darkened eucalyptus tree at the end of the promenade. I know all this, he thought, I understand all this, and, in the twilight, the eucalyptus strangely resembles a big Russian birch. Can this be the end? Such an idiotic end. . . . I feel worse and worse. . . . What's happening to me? . . . Oh my God!

About ten minutes passed, no more. His watch ticked on, trying tactfully not to look at him. The thought of death coincided precisely with the thought that in half an hour he would walk out onto the bright stage and say the first words of his part, '*Je vous prie d'excuser, Madame, cette invasion nocturne.*' And these words, clearly and elegently engraved in his memory, seemed far more real than the lapping and splashing of the weary waves, or the sound of two gay female voices coming from behind the stone wall of a nearby villa, or the recent talk of Koldunov, or even the pounding of his own heart. His feeling of sickness suddenly reached such a panicky pitch that he got up and walked along the parapet, dazedly stroking it and peering at the colored inks of the evening sea. 'In any case,' Lik said aloud, 'I have to cool off. . . . Instant cure. . . . Either I'll die or it'll help.' He slid down the sloping edge of the sidewalk, where the parapet stopped and crunched across the pebbly beach. There was nobody on the shore except for a shabbily dressed man, who happened to be lying supine near a boulder his feet spread wide apart. Something about the outline of his legs and shoulders for some reason reminded Lik of Koldunov. Swaying a little and already stooping, Lik walked self-consciously to the edge of the water, and was about to scoop some up in his hands and douse his head; but the water was alive, moving, and threatening to soak his feet. Perhaps I have enough coördination left to take off my shoes and socks, he thought, and in the same instant remembered the carton box containing his new shoes. He had forgotten it at Koldunov's!

And as soon as he remembered it, this image proved so stimulating that immediately everything was simplified, and this saved Lik, in the same way as a situation is sometimes saved by its rational formulation. He must get those shoes at once, there was just time enough to get them, and as soon as this was accomplished, he would step onstage in them. (All perfectly clear and logical.)

Forgetting the pressure in his chest, the foggy feeling, the nausea, Lik climbed back up to the promenade, and in a sonorously recorded voice hailed the empty taxi that was just leaving the curb by the villa across the way. Its brakes responded with a lacerating moan. He gave the chauffeur the address from his notebook, telling him to go as fast as possible, even though the entire trip—there and from there to the theater—would not take more than five minutes.

The taxi approached Koldunov's place from the direction of the square. A crowd had gathered, and it was only by dint of persistent threats with its horn that the driver managed to squeeze through. Koldunov's wife was sitting on a chair by the public fountain. Her forehead and left cheek glistened with blood, her hair was matted, and she sat quite straight and motionless, surrounded by the curious, while, next to her, also motionless, stood her boy, in a blood-stained shirt, covering his face with his fist, a kind of tableau. A policeman, mistaking Lik for the doctor, escorted him into the room. The dead man lay on the floor amid broken crockery, his face blasted by a gunshot in the mouth, his widespread feet in new, white——

'Those are mine,' said Lik in French.

Menton, 1938

The Vane Sisters

I might never have heard of Cynthia's death, had I not run, that night, into D., whom I had also lost track of for the last four years or so; and I might never have run into D., had I not got involved in a series of trivial investigations.

The day, a compunctious Sunday after a week of blizzards, had been part jewel, part mud. In the midst of my usual afternoon stroll through the small hilly town attached to the girls' college where I taught French literature. I had stopped to watch a family of brilliant icicles drip-dripping from the eaves of a frame house. So clear-cut were their pointed shadows on the white boards behind them that I was sure the shadows of the falling drops should be visible too. But they were not. The roof jutted too far out, perhaps, or the angle of vision was faulty, or, again, I did not chance to be watching the right icicle when the right drop fell. There was a rhythm, an alternation in the dripping that I found as teasing as a coin trick. It led me to inspect the corners of several house blocks, and this brought me to Kelly Road, and right to the house where D. used to live when he was instructor here. And as I looked up at the eaves of the adjacent garage with its full display of transparent stalactites backed by their blue silhouettes, I was rewarded at last, upon choosing one, by the sight of what might be described as the dot of an exclamation mark leaving its ordinary position to glide down very fast—a jot faster than the thaw-drop it raced. This twinned twinkle was delightful but not completely satisfying; or rather it only sharpened my appetite for other tidbits of light and shade, and I walked on in a state of raw awareness that seemed to transform the whole of my being into one big eyeball rolling in the world's socket.

Through peacocked lashes I saw the dazzling diamond reflection of the low sun on the round back of a parked automobile. To all kinds of things a vivid pictorial sense had been restored by the sponge of the thaw. Water in overlapping festoons flowed down one sloping street and turned gracefully into another. With ever so slight a note of meretricious appeal, narrow passages between buildings revealed treasures of brick and purple. I remarked for the first time the humble fluting—last echoes of grooves on the shafts of columns—ornamenting a garbage can, and I also saw the rippling upon its lid—circles diverging from a fantastically ancient center. Erect, dark-headed shapes of dead snow (left by the blades of a bulldozer last Friday) were lined up like rudimentary penguins along the curbs, above the brilliant vibration of live gutters.

I walked up, and I walked down, and I walked straight into a delicately dying sky, and finally the sequence of observed and observant things brought me, at my usual eating time, to a street so distant from my usual eating place that I decided to try a restaurant which stood on the fringe of the town. Night had fallen without sound or ceremony when I came out again. The lean ghost, the elongated umbra cast by a parking meter upon some damp snow, had a strange ruddy tinge; this I made out to be due to the tawny red light of the restaurant sign above the sidewalk; and it was then—as I sauntered there, wondering rather wearily if in the course of my return tramp I might be lucky enough to find the same in neon blue it was then that a car crunched to a standstill near me and D. got out of it with an exclamation of feigned pleasure.

He was passing, on his way from Albany to Boston, through the town he had dwelt in before, and more than once in my life have I felt that stab of vicarious emotion followed by a rush of personal irritation against travelers who seem to feel nothing at all upon revisiting spots that ought to harass them at every step with wailing and writhing memories. He ushered me back into the bar that I had just left, and after the usual exchange of buoyant platitudes came the inevitable vacuum which he filled with the random words: 'Say, I never thought there was anything wrong with Cynthia Vane's heart. My lawyer tells me she died last week.'

2

He was still young, still brash, still shifty, still married to the gentle, exquisitely pretty woman who had never learned or suspected anything about his disastrous affair with Cynthia's hysterical young sister, who in her turn had known nothing of the interview I had had with Cynthia when she suddenly summoned me to Boston to make me swear I would talk to D. and get him 'kicked out' if he did not stop seeing Sybil at once—or did not divorce his wife (whom incidentally she visualized through the prism of Sybil's wild talk as a termagant and a fright). I had cornered him immediately. He had said there was nothing to worry about—had made up his mind, anyway, to give up his college job and move with his wife to Albany where he would work in his father's firm; and the whole matter, which had threatened to become one of those hopelessly entangled situations that drag on for years, with peripheral sets of well-meaning friends endlessly discussing it in universal secrecy—and even founding, among themselves, new intimacies upon its alien woes—came to an abrupt end.

I remember sitting next day at my raised desk in the large classroom where a mid-year examination in French Lit. was being held on the eve of Sybil's suicide. She came in on high heels, with a suitcase, dumped it in a corner where several other bags were stacked, with a single shrug slipped her fur coat off her thin shoulders, folded it on her bag, and with two or three other girls stopped before my desk to ask when would I mail them their grades. It would take me a week, beginning from tomorrow, I said, to read the stuff. I also remember wondering whether D. had already informed her of his decision—and I felt acutely unhappy about my dutiful little student as during one hundred and fifty minutes my gaze kept reverting to her, so childishly slight in close-fitting gray, and kept observing that carefully waved dark hair, that small, small-flowered hat with a little hyaline veil as worn that season and under it her small face broken into a cubist pattern by scars due to a skin disease, pathetically masked by a sun-lamp tan that hardened her features whose charm was further impaired by her having painted everything that could be painted, so that the pale gums of her teeth between cherry-red chapped lips and the diluted blue ink of her eyes under darkened lids were the only visible openings into her beauty.

Next day, having arranged the ugly copybooks alphabetically, I plunged into their chaos of scripts and came prematurely to Valevsky and Vane whose books I had somehow misplaced. The first was dressed up for the occasion in a semblance of legibility, but Sybil's work displayed her usual combination of several demon hands. She had begun in very pale, very hard pencil which had conspicuously embossed the blank verso, but had produced little of permanent value on the upper-side of the page. Happily the tip soon broke, and Sybil continued in another, darker lead, gradually lapsing into the blurred thickness of what looked almost like charcoal, to which, by sucking the blunt point, she had contributed some traces of lipstick. Her work, although even poorer than I had expected, bore all the signs of a kind of desperate conscientiousness, with underscores, transposes, unnecesary footnotes, as if she were intent upon rounding up things in the most respectable manner possible. Then she had borrowed Mary Valevsky's fountain pen and added: *'Cette examain est finie ainsi que ma vie. Adieu, jeunes filles!* Please, *Monsieur le Professeur,* contact *ma sœur* and tell her that Death was not better than D minus, but definitely better than Life minus D.'

I lost no time in ringing up Cynthia who told me it was all over—had been all over since eight in the morning—and asked me to bring her the note, and when I did, beamed through her tears with proud admiration for the whimsical use ('Just like her!') Sybil had made of an examination in French literature. In no time she 'fixed' two highballs, while never parting with Sybil's notebook —by now splashed with soda water and tears—and went on studying the death message, whereupon I was impelled to point out to her the grammatical mistakes in it and to explain the way 'girl' is translated in American colleges lest students innocently bandy around the French equivalent of 'wench,' or worse. These rather tasteless trivialities pleased Cynthia hugely as she rose, with gasps, above the heaving surface of her grief. And then, holding that limp notebook as if it were a kind of passport to a casual Elysium (where pencil points do not snap and a dreamy young beauty with an impeccable complexion winds a lock of her hair on a dreamy forefinger, as she meditates over some celestial test), Cynthia led me upstairs, to a chilly little bedroom just to show me, as if I were the police or a sympathetic Irish neighbor, two empty pill bottles and the tumbled bed from which a tender, inessential body, that D. must have known down to its last velvet detail, had been already removed.

3

It was four or five months after her sister's death that
I began seeing Cynthia fairly often. By the time I had
come to New York for some vocational research in the
Public Library she had also moved to that city where for
some odd reason (in vague connection, I presume, with
artistic motives) she had taken what people, immune to
gooseflesh, term a 'cold water' flat, down in the scale of
the city's transverse streets. What attracted me were
neither her ways, which I thought repulsively vivacious,
nor her looks, which other men thought striking. She had
wide-spaced eyes very much like her sister's, of a frank,
frightened blue with dark points in a radial arrangement.
The interval between her thick black eyebrows was
always shiny, and shiny too were the fleshy volutes of
her nostrils. The coarse texture of her epiderm looked
almost masculine, and, in the stark lamplight of her
studio, you could see the pores of her thirty-two-year-old
face fairly gaping at you like something in an aquarium.
She used cosmetics with as much zest as her little sister
had, but with an additional slovenliness that would
result in her big front teeth getting some of the rouge.
She was handsomely dark, wore a not too tasteless
mixture of fairly smart heterogeneous things, and had a
so-called good figure; but all of her was curiously frowsy,
after a way I obscurely associated with left-wing en-
thusiasms in politics and 'advanced' banalities in art,
although, actually, she cared for neither. Her coily hair-
do, on a part-and-bun basis, might have looked feral and
bizarre had it not been thoroughly domesticated by its
own soft unkemptness at the vulnerable nape. Her

fingernails were gaudily painted, but badly bitten and not clean. Her lovers were a silent young photographer with a sudden laugh and two older men, brothers, who owed a small printing establishment across the street. I wondered at their tastes whenever I glimpsed, with a secret shudder, the higgledy-piggledy striation of black hairs that showed all along her pale shins through the nylon of her stockings with the scientific distinctness of a preparation flattened under glass; or when I felt, at her every movement, the dullish, stalish, not particularly conspicuous but all-pervading and depressing emanation that her seldom bathed flesh spread from under weary perfumes and creams.

Her father had gambled away the greater part of a comfortable fortune, and her mother's first husband had been of Slav origin, but otherwise Cynthia Vane belonged to a good, respectable family. For aught we know, it may have gone back to kings and soothsayers in the mists of ultimate islands. Transferred to a newer world, to a landscape of doomed, splendid deciduous trees, her ancestry presented, in one of its first phases, a white churchful of farmers against a black thunderhead, and then an imposing array of townsmen engaged in mercantile pursuits, as well as a number of learned men, such as Dr. Jonathan Vane, the gaunt bore (1780–1839), who perished in the conflagration of the steamer 'Lexington' to become later an habitué of Cynthia's tilting table. I have always wished to stand genealogy on its head, and here I have an opportunity to do so, for it is the last scion, Cynthia, and Cynthia alone, who will remain of any importance in the Vane dynasty. I am alluding of course to her artistic gift, to her delightful, gay, but not very popular paintings which the friends of her friends bought at long intervals—and I dearly should like to know where they went after her death, those honest and poetical pictures that illumined her living-room—the wonderfully detailed images of metallic things, and my favorite 'Seen Through a Windshield'—a windshield partly covered with rime, with a brilliant trickle (from an imaginary car roof) across its transparent part and, through it all, the sapphire flame of the sky and a green and white fir tree.

4

Cynthia had a feeling that her dead sister was not altogether pleased with her—had discovered by now that she and I had conspired to break her romance; and so, in order to disarm her shade, Cynthia reverted to a rather primitive type of sacrificial offering (tinged, however, with something of Sybil's humor), and began to send to D.'s business address, at deliberately unfixed dates, such trifles as snapshots of Sybil's tomb in a poor light; cuttings of her own hair which was indistinguishable from Sybil's; a New England sectional map with an inked-in cross, midway between two chaste towns, to mark the spot where D. and Sybil had stopped on October the twenty-third, in broad daylight, at a lenient motel, in a pink and brown forest; and, twice, a stuffed skunk.

Being as a conversationalist more voluble than explicit, she never could describe in full the theory of intervenient auras that she had somehow evolved. Fundamentally there was nothing particularly new about her private creed since it presupposed a fairly conventional hereafter, a silent solarium of immortal souls (spliced with mortal antecedents) whose main recreation consisted of periodical hoverings over the dear quick. The interesting point was a curious practical twist that Cynthia gave to her tame metaphysics. She was sure that her existence was influenced by all sorts of dead friends each of whom took turns in directing her fate much as if she were a stray kitten which a schoolgirl in passing gathers up, and presses to her cheek, and carefully puts

down again, near some suburban hedge—to be stroked
presently by another transient hand or carried off to a
world of doors by some hospitable lady.

For a few hours, or for several days in a row, and
sometimes recurrently, in an irregular series, for months
or years, anything that happened to Cynthia, after a
given person had died, would be, she said, in the manner
and mood of that person. The event might be extraordinary, changing the course of one's life; or it might be a
string of minute incidents just sufficiently clear to stand
out in relief against one's usual day and then shading off
into still vaguer trivia as the aura gradually faded. The
influence might be good or bad; the main thing was that
its source could be identified. It was like walking
through a person's soul, she said. I tried to argue that
she might not always be able to determine the exact
source since not everybody has a recognizable soul; that
there are anonymous letters and Christmas presents
which anybody might send; that, in fact, what Cynthia
called 'a usual day' might be itself a weak solution of
mixed auras or simply the routine shift of a humdrum
guardian angel. And what about God? Did or did not
people who would resent any omnipotent dictator on
earth look forward to one in heaven? And wars? What a
dreadful idea—dead soldiers still fighting with living
ones, or phantom armies trying to get at each other
through the lives of crippled old men.

But Cynthia was above generalities as she was beyond
logic. 'Ah, that's Paul,' she would say when the soup
spitefully boiled over, or: 'I guess good Betty Brown is
dead'—when she won a beautiful and very welcome

vacuum cleaner in a charity lottery. And, with Jamesian meanderings that exasperated my French mind, she would go back to a time when Betty and Paul had not yet departed, and tell me of the showers of well-meant, but odd and quite unacceptable bounties—beginning with an old purse that contained a check for three dollars which she picked up in the street and, of course, returned (to the aforesaid Betty Brown—this is where she first comes in—a decrepit colored woman hardly able to walk), and ending with an insulting proposal from an old beau of hers (this is where Paul comes in) to paint 'straight' pictures of his house and family for a reasonable remuneration—all of which followed upon the demise of a certain Mrs. Page, a kindly but petty old party who had pestered her with bits of matter-of-fact advice since Cynthia had been a child.

Sybil's personality, she said, had a rainbow edge as if a little out of focus. She said that had I known Sybil better I would have at once understood how Sybil-like was the aura of minor events which, in spells, had suffused her, Cynthia's, existence after Sybil's suicide. Ever since they had lost their mother they had intended to give up their Boston home and move to New York, where Cynthia's paintings, they thought, would have a chance to be more widely admired; but the old home had clung to them with all its plush tentacles. Dead Sybil, however, had proceeded to separate the house from its view—a thing that affects fatally the sense of home. Right across the narrow street a building project had come into loud, ugly, scaffolded life. A pair of familiar poplars died that spring, turning to blond skeletons. Workmen came and broke up the warm-colored lovely old sidewalk that had a special violet sheen on wet April days and had echoed so memorably to the morning footsteps of museum-bound Mr. Lever, who upon retiring from business at sixty had devoted a full quarter of a century exclusively to the study of snails.

Speaking of old men, one should add that sometimes these posthumous auspices and interventions were in the nature of parody. Cynthia had been on friendly terms with an eccentric librarian called Porlock who in the last years of his dusty life had been engaged in examining old books for miraculous misprints such as the substitution of 'l' for the second 'h' in the word 'hither.' Contrary to Cynthia, he cared nothing for the thrill of obscure predictions; all he sought was the freak itself, the chance that mimics choice, the flaw that looks like a flower; and Cynthia, a much more perverse amateur of mis-shapen or illicitly connected words, puns, logogriphs, and so on, had helped the poor crank to pursue a quest that in the light of the example she cited struck me as statistically insane. Anyway, she said, on the third day after his death she was reading a magazine and had just come across a quotation from an imperishable poem (that she, with other gullible readers, believed to have been really composed in a dream) when it dawned upon her that 'Alph' was a prophetic sequence of the initial letters of Anna Livia Plurabelle (another sacred river running through, or rather around, yet another fake dream), while the additional 'h' modestly stood, as a private signpost, for the word that had so hypnotized Mr. Porlock. And I wish I could recollect that novel or short story (by some contemporary writer, I believe) in which, unknown to its author, the first letters of the words in its last paragraph formed, as deciphered by Cynthia, a message from his dead mother.

5

I am sorry to say that not content with these ingenious fancies Cynthia showed a ridiculous fondness for spiritualism. I refused to accompany her to sittings in which paid mediums took part: I knew too much about that from other sources. I did consent, however, to attend little farces rigged up by Cynthia and her two poker-faced gentlemen-friends of the printing shop. They were podgy, polite, and rather eerie old fellows, but I satisfied myself that they possessed considerable wit and culture. We sat down at a light little table, and crackling tremors started almost as soon as we laid our fingertips upon it. I was treated to an assortment of ghosts who rapped out their reports most readily though refusing to elucidate anything that I did not quite catch. Oscar Wilde came in and in rapid garbled French, with the usual anglicisms, obscurely accused Cynthia's dead parents of what appeared in my jottings as '*plagiatisme.*' A brisk spirit contributed the unsolicited information that he, John Moore, and his brother Bill had been coal miners in Colorado and had perished in an avalanche at 'Crested Beauty' in January 1883. Frederic Myers, an old hand at the game, hammered out a piece of verse (oddly resembling Cynthia's own fugitive productions) which in part reads in my notes:

> *What is this—a conjuror's rabbit,*
> *Or a flawy but genuine gleam—*
> *Which can check the perilous habit*
> *And dispel the dolorous dream?*

Finally, with a great crash and all kinds of shudderings and jig-like movements on the part of the table, Leo Tolstoy visited our little group and, when asked to identify himself by specific traits of terrene habitation, launched upon a complex description of what seemed to be some Russian type of architectural woodwork ('figures on boards—man, horse, cock, man, horse, cock'), all of which was difficult to take down, hard to understand, and impossible to verify.

I attended two or three other sittings which were even sillier but I must confess that I preferred the childish entertainment they afforded and the cider we drank (Podgy and Pudgy were teetotallers) to Cynthia's awful house parties.

She gave them at the Wheelers' nice flat next door—the sort of arrangement dear to her centrifugal nature, but then, of course, her own living-room always looked like a dirty old palette. Following a barbaric, unhygienic, and adulterous custom, the guests' coats, still warm on the inside, were carried by quiet, baldish Bob Wheeler into the sanctity of a tidy bedroom and heaped on the conjugal bed. It was also he who poured out the drinks which were passed around by the young photographer while Cynthia and Mrs. Wheeler took care of the canapés.

A late arrival had the impression of lots of loud people unnecessarily grouped within a smoke-blue space between two mirrors gorged with reflections. Because, I suppose, Cynthia wished to be the youngest in the room, the women she used to invite, married or single, were, at the best, in their precarious forties; some of them would bring from their homes, in dark taxis, intact vestiges of good looks, which, however, they lost as the party progressed. It has always amazed me—the capacity sociable week-end revelers have of finding almost at once, by a purely empiric but very precise method, a common denominator of drunkenness, to which everybody loyally sticks before descending, all together, to the next level. The rich friendliness of the matrons was marked by tomboyish overtones, while the fixed inward look of amiably tight men was like a sacrilegious parody of pregnancy. Although some of the guests were connected in one way or another with the arts, there was no inspired talk, no wreathed, elbow-propped heads, and of course no flute girls. From some vantage point where she had been sitting in a stranded mermaid pose on the pale carpet with one or two younger fellows, Cynthia, her face varnished with a film of beaming sweat, would creep up on her knees, a proffered plate of nuts in one hand, and crisply tap with the other the athletic leg of Cochran or Corcoran, an art dealer, ensconced, on a pearl-gray sofa, between two flushed, happily disintegrating ladies.

At a further stage there would come spurts of more riotous gaiety. Corcoran or Coransky would grab Cynthia or some other wandering woman by the shoulder and lead her into a corner to confront her with a grinning embroglio of private jokes and rumors, whereupon, with a laugh and a toss of her head, she would break away. And still later there would be flurries of intersexual chumminess, jocular reconciliations, a bare fleshy arm flung around another woman's husband (he standing very upright in the midst of a swaying room), or a sudden rush of flirtatious anger, of clumsy pursuit—

and the quiet half smile of Bob Wheeler picking up
glasses that grew like mushrooms in the shade of chairs.

After one last party of that sort, I wrote Cynthia a
perfectly harmless and, on the whole, well-meant note, in
which I poked a little Latin fun at some of her guests. I
also apologized for not having touched her whisky, saying that as a Frenchman I preferred the grape to the
grain. A few days later I met her on the steps of the
Public Library, in the broken sun, under a weak cloud-
burst, opening her amber umbrella, struggling with a
couple of armpitted books (of which I relieved her for a
moment). 'Footfalls on the Boundary of Another World,'
by Robert Dale Owen, and something on 'Spiritualism
and Christianity'; when, suddenly, with no provocation
on my part, she blazed out at me with vulgar vehemence,
using poisonous words, saying—through pear-shaped
drops of sparse rain—that I was a prig and a snob; that
I only saw the gestures and disguises of people; that
Corcoran had rescued from drowning, in two different
oceans, two men—by an irrelevant coincidence both
called Corcoran; that romping and screeching Joan Winter had a little girl doomed to grow completely blind in a
few months; and that the woman in green with the
freckled chest whom I had snubbed in some way or
other had written a national best-seller in 1932. Strange
Cynthia! I had been told she could be thunderously rude
to people whom she liked and respected; one had, however, to draw the line somewhere and since I had by then
sufficiently studied her interesting auras and other odds
and ids, I decided to stop seeing her altogether.

6

The night D. informed me of Cynthia's death I returned after eleven to the two-storied house I shared, in horizontal section, with an emeritus professor's widow. Upon reaching the porch I looked with the apprehension of solitude at the two kinds of darkness in the two rows of windows: the darkness of absence and the darkness of sleep.

I could do something about the first but could not duplicate the second. My bed gave me no sense of safety; its springs only made my nerves bounce. I plunged into Shakespeare's sonnets—and found myself idiotically checking the first letters of the lines to see what sacramental words they might form. I got fate (LXX), ATOM (CXX) and twice, TAFT (LXXXVIII, CXXXI). Every now and then I would glance around to see how the objects in my room were behaving. It was strange to think that if bombs began to fall I would feel little more than a gambler's excitement (and a great deal of earthy relief) whereas my heart would burst if a certain suspiciously tense-looking little bottle on yonder shelf moved a fraction of an inch to one side. The silence, too, was suspiciously compact as if deliberately forming a black back-drop for the nerve flash caused by any small sound of unknown origin. All traffic was dead. In vain did I pray for the groan of a truck up Perkins Street. The woman above who used to drive me crazy by the booming thuds occasioned by what seemed monstrous feet of stone (actually, in diurnal life, she was a small dumpy creature resembling a mummified guinea pig) would have earned my blessings had she now trudged to her bathroom. I put out my light and cleared my throat several times so as to be responsible for at least *that* sound. I thumbed a mental ride with a very remote automobile but it dropped me before I had a chance to doze off. Presently a crackle (due, I hoped, to a discarded and crushed sheet of paper opening like a mean, stubborn night flower)—started and stopped in the wastepaper basket, and my bed-table responded with a little click. It would have been just like Cynthia to put on right then a cheap poltergeist show.

I decided to fight Cynthia. I reviewed in thought the modern era of raps and apparitions, beginning with the knockings of 1848, at the hamlet of Hydesville, N.Y., and ending with grotesque phenomena at Cambridge, Mass.; I evoked the ankle-bones and other anatomical castanets of the Fox sisters (as described by the sages of the University of Buffalo); the mysteriously uniform type of delicate adolescent in bleak Epworth or Tedworth, radiating the same disturbances as in old Peru; solemn Victorian orgies with roses falling and accordions floating to the strains of sacred music; professional imposters regurgitating moist cheese-cloth; Mr. Duncan, a lady medium's dignified husband, who, when asked if he would submit to a search, excused himself on the ground of soiled underwear; old Alfred Russel Wallace, the naïve naturalist, refusing to believe that the white form with bare feet and unperforated ear-lobes before him, at a private pandemonium in Boston, could be prim Miss Cook whom he had just seen asleep, in her curtained corner, all dressed in black, wearing laced-up boots and earrings; two other investigators, small, puny, but reasonably intelligent and active men, closely clinging

with arms and legs about Eusapia, a large, plump elderly
female reeking of garlic, who still managed to fool them;
and the sceptical and embarrassed magician, instructed
by charming young Margery's 'control' not to get lost in
the bathrobe's lining but to follow up the left stocking
until he reached the bare thigh—upon the warm skin of
which he felt a 'teleplastic' mass that appeared to the
touch uncommonly like cold, uncooked liver.

7

I was appealing to flesh, and the corruption of flesh, to refute and defeat the possible persistence of discarnate life. Alas, these conjurations only enhanced my fear of Cynthia's phantom. Atavistic peace came with dawn, and when I slipped into sleep, the sun through the tawny window shades penetrated a dream that somehow was full of Cynthia.

This was disappointing. Secure in the fortress of daylight, I said to myself that I had expected more. She, a painter of glass-bright minutiae—and now so vague! I lay in bed, thinking my dream over and listening to the sparrows outside: Who knows, if recorded and then run backward, those bird sounds might not become human speech, voiced words, just as the latter become a twitter when reversed? I set myself to re-read my dream—backward, diagonally, up, down—trying hard to unravel something Cynthia-like in it, something strange and suggestive that must be there.

I could isolate, consciously, little. Everything seemed blurred, yellow-clouded, yielding nothing tangible. Her inept acrostics, maudlin evasions, theopathies—every recollection formed ripples of mysterious meaning. Everything seemed yellowly blurred, illusive, lost.

The Visit to the Museum

Several years ago a friend of mine in Paris—a person with oddities, to put it mildly—learning that I was going to spend two or three days at Montisert, asked me to drop in at the local museum where there hung, he was told, a portrait of his grandfather by Leroy. Smiling and spreading out his hands, he related a rather vague story to which I confess I paid little attention, partly because I do not like other people's obtrusive affairs, but chiefly because I had always had doubts about my friend's capacity to remain this side of fantasy. It went more or less as follows: after the grandfather died in their St. Petersburg house back at the time of the Russo-Japanese War, the contents of his apartment in Paris were sold at auction. The portrait, after some obscure peregrinations, was acquired by the museum of Leroy's native town. My friend wished to know if the portrait was really there; if there, if it could be ransomed; and if it could, for what price. When I asked why he did not get in touch with the museum, he replied that he had written several times, but had never received an answer.

I made an inward resolution not to carry out the request—I could always tell him I had fallen ill or changed my itinerary. The very notion of seeing sights, whether they be museums or ancient buildings, is loathsome to me; besides, the good freak's commission seemed absolute nonsense. It so happened, however, that, while wandering about Montisert's empty streets in search of a stationery store, and cursing the spire of a long-necked cathedral, always the same one, that kept popping up at the end of every street, I was caught in a violent downpour which immediately went about accelerating the fall of the maple leaves, for the fair weather of a southern October was holding on by a mere thread. I dashed for cover and found myself on the steps of the museum.

It was a building of modest proportions, constructed of many-colored stones, with columns, a gilt inscription over the frescoes of the pediment, and a lion-legged stone bench on either side of the bronze door. One of its leaves stood open, and the interior seemed dark against the shimmer of the shower. I stood for a while on the steps, but, despite the overhanging roof, they were gradually growing speckled. I saw that the rain had set in for good, and so, having nothing better to do, I decided to go inside. No sooner had I trod on the smooth, resonant flagstones of the vestibule than the clatter of a moved stool came from a distant corner, and the custodian—a banal pensioner with an empty sleeve—rose to meet me, laying aside his newspaper and peering at me over his spectacles. I paid my franc and, trying not to look at some statues at the entrance (which were as traditional and as insignificant as the first number in a circus program), I entered the main hall.

Everything was as it should be: gray tints, the sleep of substance, matter dematerialized. There was the usual case of old, worn coins resting in the inclined velvet of their compartments. There was, on top of the case, a pair of owls, Eagle Owl and Long-eared, with their French names reading 'Grand Duke' and 'Middle Duke' if translated. Venerable minerals lay in their open graves of dusty papier-mâché; a photograph of an astonished gentleman with a pointed beard dominated an assortment of strange black lumps of various sizes. They bore a great resemblance to frozen frass, and I paused involuntarily over them for I was quite at a loss to guess their nature, composition and function. The custodian had been following me with felted steps, always keeping a respectful distance; now, however, he came up, with one hand behind his back and the ghost of the other in his pocket, and gulping, if one judged by his Adam's apple.

'What are they?' I asked.

'Science has not yet determined,' he replied, undoubtedly having learned the phrase by rote. 'They were found,' he continued in the same phony tone, 'in 1895, by Louis Pradier, Municipal Councillor and Knight of the Legion of Honor,' and his trembling finger indicated the photograph.

'Well and good,' I said, 'but who decided, and why, that they merited a place in the museum?'

'And now I call your attention to this skull!' the old man cried energetically, obviously changing the subject.

'Still, I would be interested to know what they are made of,' I interrupted.

'Science ...' he began anew, but stopped short and looked crossly at his fingers, which were soiled with dust from the glass.

I proceeded to examine a Chinese vase, probably brought back by a naval officer; a group of porous fossils; a pale worm in clouded alcohol; a red-and-green map of Montisert in the seventeenth century; and a trio of rusted tools bound by a funereal ribbon—a spade, a mattock, and a pick. 'To dig in the past,' I thought absentmindedly, but this time did not seek clarification from the custodian, who was following me noiselessly and meekly, weaving in and out among the display cases. Beyond the first hall there was another, apparently the last, and in its center a large sarcophagus stood like a dirty bathtub, while the walls were hung with paintings.

At once my eye was caught by the portrait of a man between two abominable landscapes (with cattle and 'atmosphere'). I moved closer and, to my considerable amazement, found the very object whose existence had hitherto seemed to me but the figment of an unstable mind. The man, depicted in wretched oils, wore a frock-coat, whiskers and a large pince-nez on a cord; he bore a likeness to Offenbach, but in spite of the work's vile conventionality, I had the feeling one could make out in his features the horizon of a resemblance, as it were, to my friend. In one corner, meticulously traced in carmine against a black background, was the signature *Leroy* in a hand as commonplace as the work itself.

I felt a vinegarish breath near my shoulder, and turned to meet the custodian's kindly gaze. 'Tell me,' I asked, 'supposing someone wished to buy one of these paintings, whom should he see?'

'The treasures of the museum are the pride of the city,' replied the old man, 'and pride is not for sale.'

Fearing his eloquence, I hastily concurred, but nevertheless asked for the name of the museum's director. He tried to distract me with the story of the sarcophagus, but I insisted. Finally he gave me the name of one M. Godard and explained where I could find him.

Frankly, I enjoyed the thought that the portrait existed. It is fun to be present at the coming true of a dream, even if it is not one's own. I decided to settle the matter without delay. When I get in the spirit, no one can hold me back. I left the museum with a brisk, resonant step, and found that the rain had stopped, blueness had spread across the sky, a woman in besplattered stockings was spinning along on a silver-shining bicycle, and only over the surrounding hills did clouds still hang. Once again the cathedral began playing hide-and-seek with me, but I outwitted it. Barely escaping the onrushing tires of a furious red bus packed with singing youths, I crossed the asphalt thoroughfare and a minute later was ringing at the garden gate of M. Godard. He turned out to be a thin, middle-aged gentleman in high collar and dickey, with a pearl in the knot of his tie, and a face very much resembling a Russian wolfhound; as if that were not enough, he was licking his chops in a most doglike manner, while sticking a stamp on an envelope, when I entered his small but lavishly furnished room with its malachite inkstand on the desk and a strangely familiar Chinese vase on the mantel. A pair of fencing foils hung crossed over the mirror, which reflected the narrow gray back of his head. Here and there photographs of a warship pleasantly broke up the blue flora of the wallpaper.

'What can I do for you?' he asked, throwing the letter he had just sealed into the wastebasket. This act seemed unusual to me; however, I did not see fit to interfere. I explained in brief my reason for coming, even naming the substantial sum with which my friend was willing to part, though he had asked me not to mention it, but wait instead for the museum's terms.

'All this is delightful,' said M. Godard. 'The only thing

is, you are mistaken—there is no such picture in our museum.'

'What do you mean there is no such picture? I have just seen it! Portrait of a Russian nobleman, by Gustave Leroy.'

'We do have one Leroy,' said M. Godard when he had leafed through an oilcloth notebook and his black finger-nail had stopped at the entry in question. 'However, it is not a portrait but a rural landscape: The Return of the Herd.'

I repeated that I had seen the picture with my own eyes five minutes before and that no power on earth could make me doubt its existence.

'Agreed,' said M. Godard, 'but I am not crazy either. I have been curator of our museum for almost twenty years now and know this catalog as well as I know the Lord's Prayer. It says here Return of the Herd and that means the herd is returning, and, unless perhaps your friend's grandfather is depicted as a shepherd, I cannot conceive of his portrait's existence in our museum.'

'He is wearing a frock-coat,' I cried. 'I swear he is wearing a frock-coat!'

'And how did you like our museum in general?' M. Godard asked suspiciously. 'Did you appreciate the sar-cophagus?'

'Listen,' I said (and I think there was already a tremor in my voice), 'do me a favor—let's go there this minute, and let's make an agreement that if the portrait is there, you will sell it.'

'And if not?' inquired M. Godard.

'I shall pay you the sum anyway.'

'All right,' he said. 'Here, take this red-and-blue pencil

and using the red—the red, please—put it in writing for me.'

In my excitement I carried out his demand. Upon glancing at my signature, he deplored the difficult pronunciation of Russian names. Then he appended his own signature and, quickly folding the sheet, thrust it into his wasitcoat pocket.

'Let's go,' he said freeing a cuff.

On the way he stepped into a shop and bought a bag of sticky looking caramels which he began offering me insistently; when I flatly refused, he tried to shake out a couple of them into my hand. I pulled my hand away. Several caramels fell on the sidewalk; he stopped to pick them up and then overtook me at a trot. When we drew near the museum we saw the red tourist bus (now empty) parked outside.

'Aha,' said M. Godard, pleased. 'I see we have many visitors today.'

He doffed his hat and, holding it in front of him, walked decorously up the steps.

All was not well at the museum. From within issued rowdy cries, lewd laughter, and even what seemed like the sound of a scuffle. We entered the first hall; there the elderly custodian was restraining two sacrilegists who wore some kind of festive emblems in their lapels and were altogether very purple-faced and full of pep as they tried to extract the municipal councillor's merds from beneath the glass. The rest of the youths, members of some rural athletic organization, were making noisy fun, some of the worm in alcohol, others of the skull. One joker was in rapture over the pipes of the steam radiator, which he pretended was an exhibit; another was taking

aim at an owl with his fist and forefinger. There were
about thirty of them in all, and their motion and voices
created a condition of crush and thick noise.

M. Godard clapped his hands and pointed at a sign
reading 'Visitors to the Museum must be decently
attired.' Then he pushed his way, with me following, into
the second hall. The whole company immediately
swarmed after us. I steered Godard to the portrait; he
froze before it, chest inflated, and then stepped back a
bit, as if admiring it, and his feminine heel trod on
somebody's foot.

'Splendid picture,' he exclaimed with genuine
sincerity. 'Well, let's not be petty about this. You were
right, and there must be an error in the catalog.'

As he spoke, his fingers, moving as it were on their
own, tore up our agreement into little bits which fell like
snowflakes into a massive spittoon.

'Who's the old ape?' asked an individual in a striped
jersey, and, as my friend's grandfather was depicted
holding a glowing cigar, another funster took out a
cigarette and prepared to borrow a light from the portrait.

'All right, let us settle on the price,' I said, 'and, in any
case, let's get out of here.'

'Make way, please!' shouted M. Godard, pushing
aside the curious.

There was an exit, which I had not noticed previously,
at the end of the hall and we thrust our way through to
it.

'I can make no decision,' M. Godard was shouting
above the din. 'Decisiveness is a good thing only when
supported by law. I must first discuss the matter with the

mayor, who has just died and has not yet been elected. I doubt that you will be able to purchase the portrait but nonetheless I would like to show you still other treasures of ours.'

We found ourselves in a hall of considerable dimensions. Brown books, with a half-baked look and coarse, foxed pages, lay open under glass on a long table. Along the walls stood dummy soldiers in jack-boots with flared tops.

'Come, let's talk it over,' I cried out in desperation, trying to direct M. Godard's evolutions to a plush-covered sofa in a corner. But in this I was prevented by the custodian. Flailing his one arm, he came running after us, pursued by a merry crowd of youths, one of whom had put on his head a copper helmet with a Rembrandtesque gleam.

'Take it off, take it off!' shouted M. Godard, and someone's shove made the helmet fly off the hooligan's head with a clatter.

'Let us move on,' said M. Godard, tugging at my sleeve, and we passed into the section of Ancient Sculpture.

I lost my way for a moment among some enormous marble legs, and twice ran around a giant knee before I again caught sight of M. Godard, who was looking for me behind the white ankle of a neighboring giantess. Here a person in a bowler, who must have clambered up her, suddenly fell from a great height to the stone floor. One of his companions began helping him up, but they were both drunk, and, dismissing them with a wave of the hand, M. Godard rushed on to the next room, radiant with Oriental fabrics; there hounds raced across azure carpets, and a bow and quiver lay on a tiger skin.

Strangely, though, the expanse and motley only gave me a feeling of oppressiveness and imprecision, and, perhaps because new visitors kept dashing by or perhaps because I was impatient to leave the unnecessarily spreading museum and amid calm and freedom conclude my business negotiations with M. Godard, I began to experience a vague sense of alarm. Meanwhile we had transported ourselves into yet another hall, which must have been really enormous, judging by the fact that it housed the entire skeleton of a whale, resembling a frigate's frame; beyond were visible still other halls, with the oblique sheen of large paintings, full of storm clouds, among which floated the delicate idols of religious art in blue and pink vestments; and all this resolved itself in an abrupt turbulence of misty draperies, and chandeliers came aglitter and fish with translucent frills meandered through illuminated aquariums. Racing up a staircase, we saw, from the gallery above, a crowd of gray-haired people with umbrellas examining a gigantic mock-up of the universe.

At last, in a somber but magnificent room dedicated to the history of steam machines, I managed to halt my carefree guide for an instant.

'Enough!' I shouted, 'I'm leaving. We'll talk tomorrow.'

He had already vanished. I turned and saw, scarcely an inch from me, the lofty wheels of a sweaty locomotive. For a long time I tried to find the way back among models of railroad stations. How strangely glowed the violet signals in the gloom beyond the fan of wet tracks, and what spasms shook my poor heart! Suddenly everything changed again: in front of me stretched an infinitely long passage, containing numerous office cabinets and elusive, scurrying people. Taking a sharp turn, I found myself amid a thousand musical instruments; the walls, all mirror, reflected an enfilade of grand pianos, while in the center there was a pool with a bronze Orpheus atop a green rock. The aquatic theme did not end here as, racing back, I ended up in the Section of Fountains and Brooks, and it was difficult to walk along the winding, slimy edges of those waters.

Now and then, on one side or the other, stone stairs, with puddles on the steps, which gave me a strange sensation of fear, would descend into misty abysses, whence issued whistles, the rattle of dishes, the clatter of typewriters, the ring of hammers and many other sounds, as if, down there, were exposition halls of some kind or other, already closing or not yet completed. Then I found myself in darkness and kept bumping into unknown furniture until I finally saw a red light and walked out onto a platform that clanged under me—and suddenly, beyond it, there was a bright parlor, tastefully furnished in Empire style, but not a living soul, not a living soul. . . . By now I was indescribably terrified, but every time I turned and tried to retrace my steps along the passages, I found myself in hitherto unseen places— a greenhouse with hydrangeas and broken windowpanes with the darkness of artificial night showing through beyond; or a deserted laboratory with dusty alembics on its tables. Finally I ran into a room of some sort with coatracks monstrously loaded down with black coats and astrakhan furs; from beyond a door came a burst of

applause, but when I flung the door open, there was no
theater, but only a soft opacity and splendidly counter-
feited fog with the perfectly convincing blotches of indistinct streetlights. More than convincing! I advanced,
and immediately a joyous and unmistakable sensation of
reality at last replaced all the unreal trash amid which I
had just been dashing to and fro. The stone beneath my
feet was real sidewalk, powdered with wonderfully frag-
rant, newly fallen snow in which the infrequent pedes-
trians had already left fresh black tracks. At first the
quiet and the snowy coolness of the night, somehow
strikingly familiar, gave me a pleasant feeling after my
feverish wanderings. Trustfully, I started to conjecture
just where I had come out, and why the snow, and what
were those lights exaggeratedly but indistinctly beaming
here and there in the brown darkness. I examined and,
stooping, even touched a round spur stone on the curb,
then glanced at the palm of my hand, full of wet granu-
lar cold, as if hoping to read an explanation there. I felt
how lightly, how naïvely I was clothed, but the distinct
realization that I had escaped from the museum's maze
was still so strong that, for the first two or three minutes,
I experienced neither surprise nor fear. Continuing my
leisurely examination, I looked up at the house beside
which I was standing and was immediately struck by the
sight of iron steps and railings that descended into the
snow on their way to the cellar. There was a twinge in
my heart, and it was with a new, alarmed curiosity that I
glanced at the pavement, at its white cover along which
stretched black lines, at the brown sky across which
there kept sweeping a mysterious light, and at the massive parapet some distance away. I sensed that there was

a drop beyond it; something was creaking and gurgling
down there. Further on, beyond the murky cavity,
stretched a chain of fuzzy lights. Scuffling along the
snow in my soaked shoes, I walked a few paces, all the
time glancing at the dark house on my right; only in a
single window did a lamp glow softly under its green-
glass shade. Here, a locked wooden gate.... There, what
must be the shutters of a sleeping shop.... And by the
light of a streetlamp whose shape had long been shouting to me its impossible message, I made out the ending
of a sign—'... *inka Sapog*' ('... *oe Repair*')—but no, it
was not the snow that had obliterated the 'hard sign' at
the end. 'No, no, in a minute I shall wake up,' I said
aloud, and, trembling, my heart pounding, I turned,
walked on, stopped again. From somewhere came the
receding sound of hooves, the snow sat like a skullcap on
a slightly leaning spur stone, and indistinctly showed
white on the woodpile on the other side of the fence, and
already I knew, irrevocably, where I was. Alas, it was
not the Russia I remembered, but the factual Russia of
today, forbidden to me, hopelessly slavish, and hopelessly my own native land. A semiphantom in a light
foreign suit, I stood on the impassive snow of an October night, somewhere on the Moyka or the Fontanka
Canal, or perhaps on the Obvodny, and I had to do
something, go somewhere, run, desperately protect my
fragile, illegal life. Oh, how many times in my sleep I
had experienced a similar sensation! Now, though, it
was reality. Everything was real—the air that seemed to
mingle with scattered snowflakes, the still unfrozen
canal, the floating fish house, and that peculiar square-
ness of the darkened and the yellow windows. A man in

a fur cap, with a briefcase under his arm, came toward me out of the fog, gave me a startled glance, and turned to look again when he had passed me. I waited for him to disappear and then, with a tremendous haste, began pulling out everything I had in my pockets, ripping up papers, throwing them into the snow and stamping them down. There were some documents, a letter from my sister in Paris, five-hundred francs, a handkerchief, cigarettes; however, in order to shed all the integument of exile, I would have to tear off and destroy my clothes, my linen, my shoes, everything, and remain ideally naked; and, even though I was already shivering from my anguish and from the cold, I did what I could.

But enough. I shall not recount how I was arrested, nor tell of my subsequent ordeals. Suffice it to say that it cost me incredible patience and effort to get back aboard, and that, ever since, I have foresworn carrying out commissions entrusted one by the insanity of others.

Other Panthers For Your Enjoyment

Some Continentals

☐ **Roger Peyrefitte**   **THE JEWS**   50p
Lovely Osmonde shocks her family because she wants to marry a
Jew – but as the witty author scarifyingly shows: if she can't marry
someone with Jewish blood . . . there may well be no-one left she
can marry.

☐ **Robert Musil**   **YOUNG TORLESS**   30p
A homosexual novel from one of Europe's great modern writers
about four cadets enmeshed in the machinery of a Teutonic military
academy. The systematic bullying that only too often degenerates
into torture is horrifying reading. 'I strongly recommend it' – *Punch*

☐ **Jean-Paul Sartre**   **INTIMACY**   30p
Ranges over the whole field of today's arid spirituality, from the
anguished conflict between 'love' and 'sex' to the feverish childhood
of a fascist rabble-rouser-to-be. A key book to modern life.

☐ **Agnar Mykle**   **LASSO ROUND**
                                         THE MOON   30p
The multi-million-selling novel of Scandinavian youth and sex.

☐ **Alberto Moravia**   **COMMAND AND I**
                                       WILL OBEY YOU   30p
Twenty-seven short-short razor-sharp stories by the world-famous
author of THE WOMAN OF ROME. 'One of the greatest living
writers, and this volume is a harsh, pungent, delicious pleasure' –
New Statesman

☐ **Hermann Hesse**   **DEMIAN**   30p
Hesse has become a modern 'cult' figure. DEMIAN, eerily mystical,
deals with the progress of a confused young man to some sort of
final enlightment – which is achieved on a hallucinatory World
War I battlefield in the novel's climactic last chapter. DEMIAN is
already in its fourth Panther Books edition.

Bestselling Classics

☐ **Homer (trans. Robert Fitzgerald)   THE ODYSSEY   50p**
The surge and thunder of the greatest story from the childhood
of the world. A modern, sinewy, universally acclaimed verse
translation.

☐ **Mrs. Gaskell   WIVES AND
                                      DAUGHTERS   50p**
Clandestine love and secret marriages across the Victorian class
barriers, by the classic author of CRANFORD. One of England's
purest works of fiction, and its awareness of social manoeuvring is
as meaningfully sharp now as when Mrs. Gaskell penned it.

☐ **Herman Melville   MOBY DICK   42p**
One of the greatest sea stories. Captain Ahab's obsessive hunting
down, over thousands of leagues and through months of time, of an
almost legendary white whale.

☐ **(translated by Geoffrey Wagner)   BAUDELAIRE:
                                        SELECTED POEMS   30p**
The erotic poetry (generally known as THE FLOWERS OF EVIL).
Baudelaire's original French on the lefthand pages, Geoffrey
Wagner's masterly no-holds-barred English on the right.

☐ **(translation Christopher Isherwood, BAUDELAIRE:
    introduction W. H. Auden)   INTIMATE JOURNALS 25p**
Modern poetry begins with the 1857 publication of the poetry
sequence THE FLOWERS OF EVIL. In this shockingly frank book
the poet reveals himself in terms of his life and art.

☐ **Edgar Allan Poe   BIZARRE AND
                                        ARABESQUE   25p**
A collection of unusual tales by the supreme exponent of horror.

Highly-Praised Modern Novels

☐ **John Fowles**   **THE FRENCH LIEUTENANT'S WOMAN**   **40p**

Although Fowles is an English – and *how* – writer his novel has been on the American bestseller lists for months. To read it is an experience. 'When the book's one sexual encounter takes place it's so explosive it nearly blows the top of your head off' – *New York Saturday Review*

☐ **David Caute**   **THE DECLINE OF THE WEST**   **50p**

A newly independent African state in bloody turmoil, and the world's adventurers – male and female – home in like vultures. Strong reading.

☐ **John Barth**   **THE SOT-WEED FACTOR**   **75p**

The story of a mid-eighteenth century man of fortune, told in a modern spirit by one of America's great writers. 'Most magnificent, totally scandalous' – Patrick Campbell, *The Sunday Times*

☐ **Elizabeth Bowen**   **EVA TROUT**   **35p**

'Elizabeth Bowen is a splendid artist, intelligent, generous and acutely aware, who has been telling her readers for years that love is a necessity, and that its loss or absence is the greatest tragedy man knows' – *Financial Times*

☐ **Norman Mailer**   **THE NAKED AND THE DEAD**   **60p**

The greatest novel from world war two.

☐ **Mordecai Richler**   **COCKSURE**   **35p**

Constantly reprinted by public demand. The brilliant satiric picture of a tycoon whose business and sexual appetites know no limits.

Obtainable from all booksellers and newsagents. If you have any difficulty please send purchase price plus 6p postage per book to Panther Cash Sales, P.O. Box 11, Falmouth, Cornwall.

I enclose a cheque/postal order for titles ticked above plus 6p. a book to cover postage and packing.

Name_____

Address_____
